COME, MY LITTLE

ANGEL

A NOVELLA

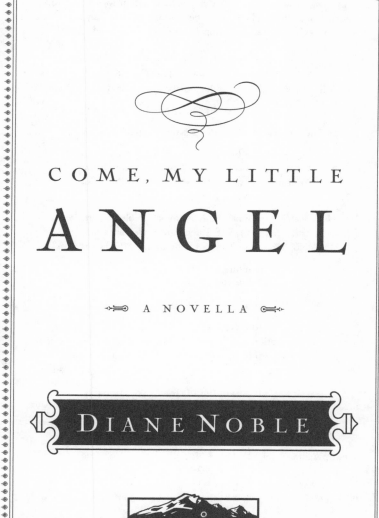

DIANE NOBLE

Multnomah® Publishers *Sisters, Oregon*

COME, MY LITTLE ANGEL
published by Multnomah Publishers, Inc.
Published in association with the literary agency of Writer's House.

International Standard Book Number: 1-57673-763-2

Cover design by The Office of Bill Chiaravalle
Cover image of Big Creek Church by Elsie Bush
Cover images by Tony Stone Images and Photodisc
Interior art by Vicki Shuck

Multnomah is a trademark of Multnomah Publishers, Inc., and
is registered in the U.S. Patent and Trademark Office.
The colophon is a trademark of Multnomah Publishers, Inc.

Scripture quotations are from:
The Holy Bible, King James Version

Printed in the United States of America

For information:
MULTNOMAH PUBLISHERS, INC.•POST OFFICE BOX 1720•SISTERS, OREGON 97759

Library of Congress Cataloging-in-Publication Data:
Noble, Diane, 1945–
  Come, my little angel / by Diane Noble.
      p. cm.   ISBN 1-57673-763-2 (pbk.)
  1. Sierra Nevada (Calif. and Nev.)–Fiction. I. Title.
PS3563.A3179765 C66 2001   813'.54–dc21   2001001644

01 02 03 04 05 06 07 08—10 9 8 7 6 5 4 3 2 1 0

This book is lovingly dedicated to the memory of my father,
one of a handful of men who, nearly fifty years ago, built
Big Creek Community Church for their families.
This little church of my childhood—nestled in the pines
of California's High Sierra—will always be my heart's compass.

And to the memory of my childhood friend, Jeanie,
the real "Littlest Angel."

Special thanks to my daughter, Amy Beth,
who at age four observed that angels
might be the real reason branches dance
when the wind blows.

CHAPTER ONE

California's Sierra Backcountry, 1912

DAISY JAMES BELIEVED in angels.

The morning the ten-year-old announced that she was certain angels lived in the pines around their clapboard cottage, her brothers Alfred and Grover, who thought themselves quite superior at ages thirteen and eleven, rolled their eyes. And her sisters—Clover, age eight, and Violet, five-going-on-six—giggled at such a notion.

With a heavy sigh Ma grabbed up baby Rosemary from her cradle by the fireplace and dropped her into the high chair in the kitchen, too busy and too tired to pay any mind to conversations about angels or anything else. Daisy could not help but hope her ma might listen this time, might give her a look that said she believed in angels too.

"I hear them whispering with the wind." Daisy stepped closer to her ma so the others could not hear. "They smile down on people who walk underneath their branches."

The baby blew oats with buzzing lips, and Ma scowled as she wiped her own nose and eyelids with the hem of her apron. "There's no such thing, child," she said to Daisy, paying attention at last. "Leastwise, not in this day and age. God helps folks that help themselves. That's why He made you able and strong." Her voice did not sound as harsh as the words did.

"Able to do for yourself. Think for yourself." She dabbed at the baby's pink cheeks with her apron, and then added, "You can't depend on magic. Or angels, either."

Daisy circled a small lock of Rosie's silken hair around one finger. "The Bible says that God's angels watch over us always. He even tells them to keep us from dashing our feet against rocks and boulders." She smiled. "I've always liked that last part. Seems to me His angels have to work extra hard in a place like Red Bud. That's why I think they're always nearby."

"Humph." Her mother poked another spoonful of oats into Rosie's mouth.

Grover hooted. "They must not be payin' God much mind. You're always stubbin' your barefoot toes in the summer."

Daisy's pa strode into the kitchen from the back of the house. His eyes crinkled at the edges as if he had been listening—and perhaps agreeing with Daisy. Just the sight of his worn, gray face turning bright for an instant warmed Daisy's heart. "Daisy girl, why all these questions about angels?"

Daisy's brothers and sisters were now crowding around the big oak table, talking and laughing while their pa served up bowls of oats and set them down with a clatter. Daisy didn't want her family to know the secret she was hiding in her heart, so she clamped her lips together and settled into the bent wood chair between Violet and Clover.

"Daisy'th alway'th talkin'th 'bout angelth." Violet, perched on a dog-eared dictionary that rested permanently in her chair, held a spoon in her fist like a small tin flag. "Alwayth and alwayth."

Clover snickered. At a warning glare from their father, Grover clapped his hand over his mouth. Even so, laughter spilled from behind his fingers.

"I suppose it's because of all the folderol she's hearing from Percival

Taggart." Ma was trying to coax another spoonful of oats through Rosie's clamped lips. "If you ask me, he needs to stick to teaching music, not filling our children's heads with such nonsense."

Pa set the last bowl of oats on the table in front of Alfred. "Heard he walked the sawdust trail in a tent meeting. Last July, I believe it was."

Violet waved her spoon. "Whath a thawdust trail?"

"Heard he gave up his whiskey," thirteen-year-old Alfred said with a know-it-all look. "But everybody says it won't last."

Grover snickered this time. "Everybody knows it's too late. I hear tell he owned the whole town before he drank it away."

Alfred let out another hoot and leaned forward, his elbows on the table. "Folks say he once played the piany in Carnegie Hall before he came to Red Bud. Now he can barely finger a fiddle."

Violet's whine rose above the clamor. "Whath a thawdust trail?"

Pa looked past her to his sons, his forehead furrowed as deep as the river canyon out yonder. "We have a rule in this household…" He did not have to finish.

All the James children knew The Rule. No matter what else they might do or say, gossip among the children was forbidden.

Grover stared at his bowl, his ears turning red. Alfred took on a grumpy, bad-tempered look that seemed to appear daily of late. But Daisy sighed, feeling some better now that the attention was turned to someone besides herself.

Violet dropped her forehead to the thum side of her fist. Her spoon clattered to the linoleum floor. "But whath a thawdust trail?"

Clover squared her shoulders. "When someone gets religion, they walk down to the front of a tent. People all around them are singin' and prayin' whilst they walk in the sawdust."

"I wanna walk in thawdust, then." Violet took a clean spoon from her father and jammed it into her bowl of oats, stirring and playing instead of eating.

Pa sighed as he sat down on the far side of Alfred. "It's a bit more complicated than that."

"Mister Taggart said his heart is different now." Daisy's voice was low, and she stared intently at the small, painted rooster on the side of her bowl. She hoped Ma and Pa would not think of her words as gossip. "He said that only God can change a person's heart."

"It's *throat* that needs changing." Grover loudly gulped a few swallows of orange juice for emphasis, followed by a loud "Aahhh." Then he stopped short at the warning frown from Pa.

"Doeth Mister Taggart believe in angelth, too?" Violet's eyes were wide.

Daisy looked up at her sister, then glanced around the table as seven pairs of eyes met hers. The only sound was a small chirping squeal Rosie made as she stuck her fingers in the oats.

Daisy bit her lip. "He says that God sends angels unawares."

"What's *that* mean?" Clover giggled. "Angels unawares."

"It means nonsense." Ma stood, her lips pressed together, and hurried to the sink. She lifted the hand pump up and down, almost like she was angry. Water dribbled out, and she dampened a cloth before heading back to the baby.

"It's in the Bible. Hebrews, chapter 13." Pa scooted his chair back from the big table. As soon as Ma finished wiping Rosie's face, he lifted the baby from her high chair and propped her thickly diapered bottom on the crook of his arm. Rosie stuck her fingers in his mouth as he quoted, "'Be not forgetful to entertain strangers; for thereby some have entertained angels unawares.'"

Daisy looked around the table as her brothers' and sisters' jaws dropped and their eyes grew round. Her heart thudded as she pondered her father's words. Did he believe in angels?

But her ma spoke again before Daisy could give the astounding thought more pondering. "I don't want our children growing up expecting angels or anybody else to rescue them from their troubles." Ma wiped her hands on her apron, then turned to the table to speak to Daisy and her sisters. Her face looked tired and drawn, and her frail shoulders slumped. "Or expecting others to take over when they should be taking care of themselves."

"I'll wash the dishes, Ma," Daisy said and rose from the table. "You go sit. Rest a spell."

"Sit?" Ma's laugh came out short and bitter as her eyes lit on the high stack of laundry at the end of the kitchen. "That's a kindly thought. But truly, child, you should know by now there's no such thing in a household such as this."

"You girls help your ma now." Pa's worried gaze drifted from Ma to Clover and Violet. "You have enough time before school to help your ma turn the wringer. Skedaddle, now."

Violet's bottom lip protruded. "But I promithed Maudie Ruth I'd meet her on the playground. We wath gonna play double-Dutch jump rope."

"Helping your mother is more important than jump rope."

"But I'm not big enough to help. I thtill thit on a book to reach the table."

Pa patted Violet's strawberry blond curls. "If you're strong enough for double-Dutch you're plenty strong enough to hand your ma the laundry."

"How come Alfred and Grover can't do it?" Clover glared at her grinning brothers, who were still sitting at the table.

Before another word was uttered, chairs teetered, wooden legs scratched the linoleum, and the boys grabbed their belt-encircled books. In one swift movement, they hoisted the straps over their backs and hurried through the screen door. It closed twice with a bang.

"It's not fair," Clover muttered. She slumped to the far end of the kitchen, punctuating her departure with a slammed door of her own. Violet followed with a loud, exasperated huff. Soon their voices, not sounding the least bit put out now, mixed with the lower tones of Ma's voice and could be heard from the small side yard.

Daisy filled the dishpan with water from the steaming kettle, sudsing it up with a bar of Fels Naptha soap as she added some cold water from the pump.

Pa still held Rosie, who was fussing now. He rocked her gently, patting her back between the shoulder blades as he leaned against the sink counter, his ankles crossed.

"You mustn't think ill of your ma, Daisy girl. About not believing in your angels, I mean."

"Do you, Pa? Believe, I mean?" She stared at the rising bubbles, not daring to look into his eyes for fear of being disappointed.

He didn't answer right away. Only the sound of Rosie sucking on her two tiny fingers was heard in the big kitchen.

"Do you?" Daisy waited to breathe until he answered.

"There are many things about God, about His angels that we don't understand. But just because we don't understand them, it doesn't mean they're not true."

Daisy turned to him and saw belief in his eyes. She almost dropped her favorite bowl with the painted rooster on the side. "You mean it?"

He smiled. "You mustn't pay too much mind to your ma's bitterness about things of God. She's had sadness in her life and that's made her afraid to believe."

Daisy rinsed the rooster bowl and carefully set it on the counter. Though it was years ago, she remembered how Ma was before the baby died…how the house was once filled with singing and laughing. Was that what her pa meant?

On his shoulder, little Rosie closed her eyes and let out a big sigh that made her chest rise. Daisy's heart filled with love for the little girl. How would she feel if Rosie were suddenly gone? A wave of sadness washed over her at the thought, and she bit her lip. If just the thought hurt this much, what must it have been like for Ma to have a baby die?

Just then the company whistle blew from across town. Pa shifted Rosie to one side, then pulled out his pocket watch. "It's time to go," he said. He strode to the old wooden cradle that sat near the fireplace and gently placed the baby inside.

Daisy's pa was big, broad shouldered. She had always imagined Paul Bunyan could not be half as strong as her pa. But watching him tuck in the sleeping Rosie, then plant a kiss on her fuzzy head, made her wonder how a big, powerful man like her pa could hold a baby with such tenderness, his face all gentlelike.

"I'll be late tonight," she heard him say to Ma a few minutes later out in the yard. "There's a meeting after work. Has to do with some blasting in tunnel number eight."

"Orin, you're not thinking of going in the tunnels again!" Ma sounded scared. "You told me you wouldn't."

Daisy stepped outside to the wide porch and looked toward the spot of brown grass near the wringer washer where they spoke. Violet and Clover had disappeared. They had most likely run off to the schoolhouse.

Daisy did not mean to eavesdrop, but the fear in her ma's voice kept her rooted to the peeling boards on the porch.

"We need the money, Abigail," her pa was saying. "There's not enough to pay the mercantile bill again. It's getting so that more goes out for food and such than I'm paid at the end of each week."

"There's got to be another way..." Ma's voice dropped, and Daisy couldn't hear the rest of her words.

"There's more," her pa said. "It's about Alfred—"

Her ma brought her hand to her mouth. "You said you wouldn't...you said you'd let him finish school. He's only *thirteen.*"

"I know I did, but circumstances are dire, Abigail. Besides, he's nearly fourteen. That's what the meeting is about. Most of us have sons who can help make ends meet. We're hoping the company will take them on. And lately his attitude, Abby, well, it's downright defiant at times..." His voice lowered, and Daisy strained to hear.

"He's so young," her ma said slightly louder.

"I was working in the mines by age twelve," Pa said. Then they turned their backs to her, and she could not hear any more. But the sad slope of their shoulders told Daisy more than any words could. Her pa wrapped one arm around her ma's thin frame and drew her close. For an instant, her ma lay her head against Pa's big chest. Then she stiffened and stood tall once more. Ma did not turn to wave when the company whistle blew again and Pa strode down the dirt road beneath the pine tree branches.

As her ma cranked the washer handle, feeding the clothes through the double rollers of the wringer, Daisy raised her eyes to the stand of sugar pines that surrounded their bleak little shack of a house.

A slight wind blew against the dark green needles, making them sway and dance, just as they might if angels were walking among the branches.

Angels! She grinned. Even Papa agreed there might be such a thing. *Think of it!*

She giggled as she considered the secret she had been holding dear. A secret that might change all the families in Red Bud. Especially her own. The secret was as precious to her as the scent of rain on a dusty summer's day. Only two people knew of it, besides herself, of course: her best friends Wren Morgan and Cady O'Leary.

Minutes later a rustling breeze kicked up her hair as she skipped along the path to the one-room schoolhouse. Shouts and laughter carried toward her as the children waited for Miss Penney to ring the school bell.

Before stepping through the rusty-hinged gate into the play yard, Daisy looked up into the canopy of pine branches. They danced and swayed and sang in the wind.

A treeful of angels, she thought with a grin. *Imagine such a thing!*

She just knew angels were around her today. This was the day she planned to tell Mister Taggart her secret. No matter what her ma or anyone else in Red Bud thought, without Mister Taggart her secret would not spring to life.

And if it did not, Daisy thought she surely might perish.

CHAPTER TWO

ABIGAIL JAMES WENT about her morning chores with a heavy heart, sweeping the kitchen floor, mending the elbows on Orin's old jacket, and kneading the bread dough she had set out at dawn to rise.

Just after Abigail sewed the last patch on Grover's trousers, Rosie began to fuss in her cradle. Abigail hurried inside, lifted the baby to her shoulder, and settled wearily into the old, scarred rocking chair near the fireplace. Rosie drank hungrily to the rhythm of the chair's movement.

Abigail leaned back, feeling the first contentment of the morning. She trailed her fingers along the worn chair arms, touching the small grooves of teething marks, some more than a decade old. She wondered which marks belonged to Alfred, or Grover, or even sweet Daisy. The little ones, Violet and Clover, had chosen a stout lamp table to soothe their swollen gums as their teeth broke through. Their marks mixed with a design of wild roses that Orin had carved around the edges when he built the piece.

Once he suggested sanding off the scars and coating the table with a new layer of shellac, but Abigail would have nothing to do with such nonsense. Unlike her neighbors, she did not long for newfangled tables and chairs and bedsteads from Sears and Roebuck in her small house. No sir. She was quite content with what she had, teeth marks and all.

Her children were furnishings enough for this thin-walled place. They looked enough alike to be six little peas fit snug in a pod, what with their freckled faces and strawberry blond hair, even the baby's, whose fuzz was just beginning to curl. But each child was special enough to fill Abigail's heart all alone. Curly-haired Violet with her giggle and lisp; Clover with pigtails that flipped and bobbed with each indignant sniff; pretty Daisy with her waist-long, swinging plaits and heart so caring that Abigail feared for the day it would surely break with disappointment, just as her own had.

And the boys…

Tears filled her eyes as she considered her earlier conversation with Orin about Alfred. How could her husband possibly be in a right state to consider sending the boy into the granite tunnels, plugging dynamite?

There would be extra pay because of the danger. That, she knew, was Orin's reasoning. Biting her trembling bottom lip, she shifted Rosie to her left side, then settled back to rock once more. True, times were hard. But it was also true that with Alfred joining Orin in the tunnels, likely Grover would be next. She had hoped for a better life for her sons. Maybe even sending them to the city for higher learning.

Orin did not have the same dreams for his sons. He had worked in the mines in West Virginia before bringing his bride and their first three babies to California back in aught one. He had vowed to make a better life for them all than the bleak existence his family had known in the mines.

Abigail stared through the window beyond the fireplace. How much better was this? Not much, by her measure. Her husband had merely traded one hole in the ground for another. He had brought them all here—Alfred, Grover, and Daisy—only to have two babies born too soon because Abigail had scarce enough to eat. When she birthed the third baby she thought God surely would not take another little one from her. But Lily died from consumption two harsh winters later.

And now this. She looked out at the tall, bleak pines around the cottage. They held out the light. Their shadows lifted too late in the mornings and returned too early in the afternoons.

She did not know exactly when her fears began and her prayers ended. She supposed it was near the day Lily died. It seemed God did not hear her prayers at all, that He paid no mind to her begging for mercy. Oh yes, she had asked Him to send His angels to guard sweet Lily, to keep her from harm…

And her precious baby had died in her arms.

The day they buried Lily in the cold, hard ground, Abigail vowed she would teach the rest of her children to fend for themselves. She determined she could not allow Daisy to believe in fairy tales or angels—in reality, they were one and the same—for one day longer. There was no sense praying, though she bowed her head respectfully when Orin led the children in prayer. Her respect was for her husband, not God.

But despite her efforts, Daisy was being duped with a dream of unseen, make-believe beings. And it was all due to the interference of Percival Taggart. Abigail's lips tightened and she choked back her anger as the rhythm of the rocker became clipped and jerking. Rosie fussed, her clear eyes steady on Abigail's.

Strangely ashamed, Abigail felt her cheeks flush. She lifted Rosie to her shoulder and patted the tiny back until a small burp erupted. Glancing up at the Liberty clock on the wall, she estimated the time that Percival Taggart worked with the children for their music lessons.

She would wait until the children were dismissed, then she would give the drunkard a piece of her mind. She would put a stop to his lies.

Smiling for the first time that morning, she cradled Rosie in her arms while "I Saw Three Ships," a song from her childhood in the Appalachian Mountains, played as if on a fairy dulcimer from someplace deep in her mind.

Oh, they sailed into Bethlehem
On Christmas Day in the morning...
And all the bells on earth shall ring
On Christmas Day, on Christmas Day,
On Christmas Day in the morning...
And all the angels in Heav'n shall sing
On Christmas Day in the morn—

Abigail grimaced when she realized her voice had been about to take flight in song. Quickly, she pushed the melody, and especially the words about singing angels, from her mind.

Seated at a tinny, upright piano, Percival Taggart nodded to the group of children, ranging from third-level to sixth-level pupils, their faces barely visible above the metal music stands.

In the front row, Daisy James, Wren Morgan, and Cady O'Leary sat on the edges of their chairs and watched him intently, awaiting his nod so they could pull their fiddle bows downward.

He played a few chords of introduction to "Amazing Grace," then nodding decisively, he struck the worn keys hard enough to show the children it was time to begin. Scratchy violins followed his lead, a few tentative horns wavered along, and a tuba blasted the wrong note a beat and a half behind the rest of the orchestra.

Flame-haired Cady O'Leary exploded with giggles. He gave her a scolding glare, but not soon enough. On either side of her, first Wren Morgan snickered, then Daisy James's cheeks turned bright red as she attempted to keep her face straight and her fiddle held parallel to the floor, just as he had taught them all.

He continued to fix his warning glare on the three, knowing the entire eleven-piece orchestra would explode into gales of laughter if he did not. And Toby McGowan the tuba player—a boy who had sprouted skyward too soon and stumbled along on feet too big for his skinny legs—would never hear the end of it.

Percival let his fingers travel over the aged ivory keys with an interlude of chords. "At the top once more, boys and girls." Another decisive nod at the downbeat, and the group was off and running again.

Except for Toby. This time his blasts bleated out three beats late.

Cady snickered more loudly than before, drawing the attention of the entire trumpet section and the single trombonist. Wren and Daisy, their shoulders quaking from silent laughter, stared at their shared music stand.

The blasts continued.

One by one the instruments drifted to a halt until the only one left playing was Toby, his cheeks puffed out, eyes closed.

Percival tapped his baton on the piano lid, then cleared his throat. "Boys and girls," he called out sternly. He rapped his baton again.

Finally, he caught their attention.

Even Toby's. The boy looked around bewildered at the now-silent room. Thankfully the children were now staring at Percival with worried faces, so he hoped Toby would not realize the laughter had been at his expense.

Just for good measure, he gave the three little girls and his other charges another warning stare. "We *all* need to work on our timing. I want you to break into groups of three or four and clap out the rhythm to the music." He named the children he wanted in each group. Scooting chairs and picking up music stands, the group dispersed.

Percival sat down with the first group: Toby, Cady, Wren, and Daisy.

❀

"Now," he said solemnly, "I want this group to beat out four-four time." He demonstrated by clapping his hands together in a four-beat rhythm. The children followed his lead. When they had it right, he stood to leave.

Daisy stopped him. "Mister Taggart, we've got something to ask you about. Something important."

Her expression tugged at his heart. He sat down again and pulled his chair forward. "About the music?"

She glanced at her friends Wren and Cady as if for support, then back to him. Toby just looked confused.

Behind them, the rest of the children were clapping merrily to imaginary beats. There was not a rhythm among them that Percival could recognize. Not four-four. Not two-four. Nothing. He sighed and turned back to the girls and Toby.

Daisy leaned closer and dropped her voice to a whisper. "We want to put on a Christmas drama show."

"About angels," Cady added. "Angels in heaven."

He smiled at the hopeful looks on their faces. So as not to disappoint them, he nodded. "Tell me more."

"Daisy wrote it herself." Wren gave her friend a proud smile.

Toby frowned, apparently still confused.

Percival looked at Daisy. "Tell me about it."

She colored a bit, her freckles fading into her flushed face. "It's for something special. Something we've been thinking about for a long time."

He nodded again to give her encouragement. "It sounds important."

"Oh, Mister Taggart—" Cady nodded, her eyes wide—"it *is*. The most important thing we've ever thought of by ourselves."

"Then tell me about it." Behind him the clapping had nearly stopped. He held up a hand to the girls and turned to the rest of the class. "Keep counting, children. One-two-three-four." He clapped hard on the first and third beats to get them started. "Now," he said, turning again to Daisy. "Why don't you tell me what you've written?"

She smiled, and hope seemed to shine through her eyes from somewhere deep in her soul. "It's called *Come, My Little Angel.*" She leaned forward and thrust a crumpled paper into his hands before rushing on. "It's about a little child who dies and goes to heaven."

"I-I've always wanted to p-play an angel." Toby McGowan looked surprised when all three little girls turned to him, their mouths gaping open. It was as if they had forgotten he still sat beside them. He shrugged. "W-well, I-I have," he stuttered. He immediately looked down at the floor, then reached for his left shoe with a grunt to fiddle with his laces.

"Your pa's the *tavern* keeper," Wren said with a haughty laugh. "What kind of an angel would *that* make?" She giggled and glanced at Cady, who rolled her eyes.

"Our angel has to be someone small," Daisy said to him, though not, Percival was glad to note, unkindly. "I mean, *much* younger. One of the first-level little ones. That's what I have in mind." She looked back to Percival as if for approval.

With a smile, Percival encouraged her to go on. "I suppose you want to put on the drama for your parents?" He glanced down at the smudged words on the paper she had given him.

She leaned closer and whispered, "You see, I have it in mind that Red Bud needs a church. People would pay to see the drama show, and that money would go to build a little church. Not a big one, like in the city. But something small. Just the right size for Red Bud."

She paused, and for a moment seemed so lost in thought he wondered if she might not continue.

"I want it to have a steeple with a bell and everything," she said reverently. "Then maybe the bell could ring instead of the company whistle, because truly, we wouldn't need the whistle anymore."

He swallowed around the sudden lump in his throat. "It sounds like you've been to such a place."

She nodded. "A long time ago and a ways from here, it was." Her voice dropped to a near whisper. "It was in such a place I last heard my ma sing. I was just a tyke, but I remember her voice was like the music of hundreds of angels' harp strings. After our baby died, she never sang again."

The child's words nearly broke Percival's heart. "A mighty big project, Daisy…" He cleared his throat, still moved by those wide, hope-filled eyes—eyes that told him Daisy believed such a church in Red Bud might bring her ma to sing again.

"I-I hate that ol' c-company whistle," Toby said. "At night it means my pa has to go to w-work 'cause all the menfolk stop by on their way home from the t-tunnels and such."

And sometimes they never make it home. Percival remembered all too well the evenings he had spent in the tavern, all too willing to keep the raucous times rolling, all too willing to keep fathers from going home to their families. A sudden thirst made him swallow hard and moisten his lips.

"Tell us more," he said at last. "About your play."

As if sensing something out of the ordinary, the other children stopped their rhythmic clapping, and the room fell quiet.

Daisy looked at her classmates, her expression uncertain.

"If you'd rather tell me later…" he said, sensing her discomfort.

"I'll tell you, if you'd like." She sat a little taller. "'Cause we'll all be working on it—if you agree to help us. I think it's time to tell."

He turned to the children, beckoning them to scoot their chairs closer.

"Daisy has written a drama about angels," he said on her behalf. "Is it a Christmas play?" He glanced at her and smiled at her beaming nod.

Then she took over, just as he had figured she would. "I have a book that I like to read to my little sister. It's called *The Littlest Angel.*" Her round eyes shone. "It's a legend about a boy who dies and goes to heaven. Only he arrives there just after Baby Jesus is born on earth. All the angels are worrying about what gifts to bring the newborn King, but the newest little angel doesn't have anything he can give—only the dearest treasures of his heart."

The children were as quiet as Percival had ever seen them.

"Th-that's a humdinger of a p-play. I wanna be the a-angel," Toby said. "The s-star angel."

The spell was broken, and the children laughed at the boy's declaration. The boys hooted, and the girls giggled.

Percival glared at his charges until they quieted down.

"I wrote a drama show about this little angel for us, for everyone," Daisy said. "It's called *Come, My Little Angel.* But I need Mister Taggart's help to figure it all out. Figure out the parts and the music."

Though something inside Percival told him not to get the little girl's hopes up, he nodded. "I can do that. And we'll need music. Songs for the children to sing."

"An angel choir!" Cady bounced up and down on her chair. "Oh yes! That will be perfect! I want to sing the solo parts."

"And an angel orchestra," Percival added, thinking of the huge task ahead.

Sighs of delight met his words, and the children jumped in with ideas about songs and lyrics. Except for the small group of sixth-level pupils in the back row. They sniffed and snickered and threw superior looks at each other.

"It's for Red Bud to build a church," Daisy said during a lull. There was a stubborn set to her chin, as if she expected opposition. "The money we make will be for that."

She wasn't wrong. Wilbur and Dwayne groaned. Thaddeus let out a snicker. The sixth-level girls tittered again, with Brooke Knight-Smyth shaking her sausage curls and rolling her eyes at her friends, Emma Jane and Edmonda. The others stared, unbelieving, at Daisy.

"Red Bud needs a church," she repeated. She clamped her lips and folded her arms as she settled back into her chair to stare back at the others.

Percival held up his hands. "Our class time is nearly over. Let's get back to our—" Just then the schoolhouse door burst open. A disheveled and angry-looking Abigail James filled the doorway, holding a fussing baby on one hip. She glanced around the room, her gaze skittering across the children's faces. Then narrowing her eyes, she turned to Percival.

"You, sir—" her soft voice quaked with emotion—"have no right to teach these impressionable minds anything other than fiddlin' lessons."

A shocked silence filled the room as she stepped closer. "I plan to speak to the school board. I'm sure they'll agree it's high time that you, Mister Taggart, be removed from your position before you can do any more damage to our children. With your drunken history in this community it should've been done a long time ago, if you ask me."

The children gasped, then a sad silence fell upon them all. It almost seemed the children had lost the ability to breathe.

As had Percival. He ripped his gaze from Abigail James's face and looked instead to her daughter. The grief in Daisy's wet eyes threatened to break his heart.

CHAPTER THREE

THE HAIR ON the back of Daisy's neck stood on end as her mother shooed the other children from the music room. A chill such as this surely meant something bad was about to happen.

"You too, Missy." Her mother gestured toward the door with her free hand while bouncing Rosie on the crook of her other arm. The baby looked at Daisy with solemn eyes. "Go on now," Daisy's mother said. "Out you go with the others."

Daisy hung her head and moved to the doorway. She stopped once to glance back, her gaze lifting briefly to meet Mister Taggart's. He gave her a slight nod, and she noticed the lines around his eyes and mouth seemed deeper and sadder than before. It struck her that his face looked like a balloon that somebody had let the air out of.

When she put her hand on the doorknob and hesitated, he said, "It's all right, Daisy. You go on now, out with the others."

From the corner of her eye, she saw her mother plant herself squarely in front of Mister Taggart. With a heavy heart, Daisy stepped outside and closed the door behind her.

The children who had been in the music room were now clustered in the play yard between the one-room schoolhouse and the small frame shack that doubled as the music room three times a week and the lunchroom on wintry days. They whispered behind their hands and watched Daisy with curious expressions. She stared back at them, unwilling to think of the shame her mother had just brought upon her, upon Mister Taggart.

Finally, Wren and Cady came closer, almost shyly, and each took one of her hands.

"It's gonna be all right, Daisy." Cady leaned her head against Daisy's shoulder.

Wren squeezed Daisy's hand. "We'll put on your drama show anyway. We don't need Mister Taggart."

"He's the one who believes...believes in angels and God helping us when we need Him. I *know* Mister Taggart's the one who could make everyone who comes to our show believe, too. I just know it." There was a sting behind her nose and eyes, and she blinked a few times and swallowed hard to make it go away.

"Maybe your ma can't really get Mister Taggart in trouble. Or maybe she'll change her mind," Cady said. But she did not sound convinced.

Daisy sighed. "My ma doesn't ever change her mind once it's made up."

Just then their teacher, Miss Penney, stepped from the schoolhouse. The pretty, flaxen-haired schoolmarm looked surprised to see the children, likely because they were not supposed to be let go from the music room before the orchestra lessons were over. Miss Penney frowned at the pocket watch that hung from a long strand of red ribbon around her neck, then she rang the handbell.

At the sound of the bell, the subdued children lined up before Miss Penney. Behind her, in the schoolhouse, sat the other half of the students that made up the twenty-seven in Red Bud school. In the last row, Daisy's sisters and brothers twisted in their seats, looking slightly pale. Had they seen their mother stomp into Mister Taggart's music room?

"Miss Penney, Miss Penney!" Cady raised her hand and hooked it behind her head, holding it in place with her other arm, elbow akimbo. She was always the first to tell anything, and Daisy sighed deeply, knowing what was coming next. "Guess what!"

Miss Penney knew Cady well, and she put her finger to her lips to shush her. "There is a time for everything, Cady. And now isn't the time for sharing your news."

Daisy heaved a sigh of relief. Perhaps Cady would not have the chance to blurt the news about her mother's visit to the class. She knew all too well the cruelty that would result. The laughter. The giggles. The wide-eyed curiosity. Not many mothers ventured on the school grounds unless it was to bring a lunch pail that a child forgot, or even less often, to bring fresh-baked cookies on a child's birthday. Not many people in Red Bud could afford such a birthday luxury, and Daisy could count the times on one hand that such a happening had taken place. Certainly, it had never happened to her or her brothers and sisters.

She marched into the schoolhouse with the other children, and only once—just before she stepped inside—did she venture a look back to the music room. But it did her no good. The door was shut. She could only imagine the scolding her mother was giving poor Mister Taggart.

She entered the room and slipped obediently into her chair. She folded her hands and, biting her lip, waited to see what would happen next. Suddenly, an idea came to her and she shot her hand into the air. "Ciphering," she almost shouted. "Let's do ciphering next."

Miss Penney had just taken her place near her desk, right in front of the blackboard. She smiled at Daisy, that puzzled frown creasing her brow again. "It's our reading time, Daisy. We will get to our multiplication tables just before lunchtime."

In the row beside her, Cady bounced up and down in her chair, making it squeak, and her hand waved in the air. "But-but-but," she stammered in her excitement, "you said you would give me time to tell you my news. Can I now?"

The other children joined in, all talking at once. Miss Penney laughed, holding up one hand. "This must be something of great importance. Everyone, quiet down now, and we'll let Cady tell us what it is."

The room fell silent, and Daisy felt tears puddle in her bottom lids. She dropped her head to her desk so nobody would see her cry. Her heart stopped as Cady began to talk.

"Well, now," Cady said with a sense of importance. "Me and my best friends Daisy and Wren have a secret. And Daisy's mama is in on it. That's why she came today. It was all, well, all part of the plan."

"My best friends and *I,"* Miss Penney corrected as confused glances were exchanged among the children who had been in the music room.

"My best friends and *I* have a secret, then," Cady said sweetly.

Immediately the room buzzed with curious chatter, and it seemed the awful scene in the music room was forgotten. Daisy drew in a deep breath and shot Cady a look of gratitude.

Cady grinned back at her as Daisy dried her tears. Over Cady's shoulder Wren beamed with approval.

Percival watched the anger fade to dismay, then to anguish, in the face of the woman in front of him.

"What you've done to our children is unforgivable. You've filled their heads with false hope." Her voice was low, overflowing with sorrow. "You have no right to plant your grand and glorious beliefs in their poor heads, making them think that life will better for them someday." She pushed back a string of limp hair with a bony hand. A hand that was created for music. He imagined her hand if her circumstances were different—slender, with tapered fingers, they would strum a harp or perhaps travel up the keys of a piano, a cuff of Irish lace or a bracelet of pearls around her wrist.

Abigail James's clothes were clean, though worn thin and patched in places. They were no different than those covering the thin frames of the other women in town. Likely she had never seen a length of lace, let alone a strand of pearls.

As though sensing his scrutiny, her cheeks turned pink. "I suppose you're lookin' down on me now?" She glanced down at her homespun skirt, and her lip curled. "I suppose now you've got religion, the rest of us aren't good enough for you? You think we're not good enough to raise our children proper? Teach them the Golden Rule?" She stepped closer, the anger sparking again in her eyes. "Is that why you've taken over, Mister Taggart?"

"Missus James—" he kept his tone calm, standing his ground—"I have done nothing of the sort. The families in Red Bud are good folks. I would argue with no one over that fact. But you must understand, the children ask me questions about life, about the unseen world. I'm merely answering their questions—and there are so many—as best I can. I don't have answers to *all* their questions." He shook his head and laughed softly. "Why, I don't even have answers to my own questions. But when they ask me, I tell them what I know."

"About God."

"Yes, sometimes."

"About angels."

"Your little Daisy doesn't seem able to put that subject to rest."

At the mention of her daughter's name, Abigail James's expression softened. "I reckon what you say is true." Then she frowned. "But if you would stop filling her mind with such nonsense, maybe then she could put it to rest."

For a moment Percival did not speak. "She's just a child. Doesn't her imagination have the right to take wing?" *Especially if those images in her heart are based on truth, not merely fairy tales?*

"Daisy's heart will only be stomped on later. I aim to protect her from that—even if it means taking on everyone who crosses her path and dares her to dream. I'll do whatever it takes to protect her."

"Such as getting me fired."

"That's my intent. I came here to warn you."

"Warn me or bargain with me?"

She stared at him without answering.

"If I stop speaking of the things in my heart, you'll not get me fired. Is that the bargain you came here to make?" He thought of Daisy's dream, her wide-eyed excitement over the play she had written…. For all her good intentions, Abigail James was about to crush her daughter's heart, to stomp on it as surely as those she swore to protect Daisy from would ever do. He considered telling the woman about Daisy's secret, but the story wasn't his to tell.

Besides, Missus James would likely blame him for placing such a notion in her daughter's head in the first place.

"If you call this a bargain instead of a warning, that's okay by me," Abigail James said, turning to leave. The baby fussed, and she soothed the little, downy head with her fingers and palm, cupping it tenderly and stroking the child's hair. The gesture was incongruous compared to the woman's harsh words. "You quit filling my children's heads with folderol, and I'll keep my mouth shut about why I think a drunkard is unfit to teach my child anything."

His breath expelled, almost as if he had been socked in the stomach. "I–I'm reformed," he managed after a moment, but the curl of her lip told him she did not believe a word of it.

"Reformed?" She laughed softly, shaking her head. "My father *reformed* himself more times than I can count. Promised my ma every Sunday that things would be different. Every Saturday night his newfangled and reformed life ended up in the gutter, and his paycheck—which was supposed to feed his family—ended up in a saloonkeeper's pocket." She laughed again, this time harshly. "That's only a portion of what I know about being reformed, Mister Taggart. I could tell you plenty more, but I'm sure you know firsthand what I'm talkin' about."

He had no defense, so did not answer. The difference between him and her father likely was not much. He drew in a deep breath as he considered her offer. This job was all he had left, all that provided him a means of support. And a small measure of dignity.

The importance of his work hit him full force. Even at his worst moments, when the slide into the gutter on a Saturday night seemed to kill everything good in his heart, it was the thought of teaching music on Monday morning that kept him going through another week.

Since last summer, when he felt God's touch as never before, when he'd promised he would not let liquor pass his lips again, he had considered his job at Red Bud school a gift for the least-deserving of the heavenly Father's creatures: Percival Taggart, town drunk. Redeemed, indeed...but oh, so fragile of flesh and spirit. His job was a gift that kept him on the straight and narrow. He couldn't give it up now. He knew too well the consequences.

He met Abigail James's cold stare. "If you want me to remain silent about these things, I shall do so, Missus James."

"Including those tall tales of God stooping down to rescue His children?"

Her words were laced with sarcasm. "Or tales of other heavenly bodies, including angels?"

"I will remain silent."

Her smile was quick and triumphant. "I thought you'd see it my way, Mister Taggart."

The door behind them opened, and a worried-looking Miss Penney burst into the room. "One of the children reported hearing raised voices just now. If there's been an altercation…" She looked first to Percival, then moved her gaze to Abigail James, who smiled and shook her head.

"No, ma'am. No altercation at all. Me and Mister Taggart just had some things to straighten out, that's all. Isn't that right, Mister Taggart?" She shot him a conspiratorial glance. "Isn't it, now?"

Miss Penney did not look convinced. "The children said you rushed in here at the end of the music lesson—"

Abigail James held up a hand to stop Miss Penney, and then, squaring her thin shoulders, she looked to Percival. "It was a misunderstanding, that's all. But we've straightened it out."

"Yes—" Percival shifted his gaze uncomfortably—"we have."

Missus James headed to the door, the baby propped on one hip, then hesitated and turned to look at Miss Penney. "You can tell the children that everything is fine. We've truly cleared up our differences."

After the two women left, Percival turned to collect the music from the children's lesson. Slowly he stacked the sheets and dropped them into the piano bench. He moved around the room, folding the music stands and carrying them to the corner of the room. When all was straightened and ready for the next lesson, he dropped to the piano bench.

For a long while he sat there, his head in his hands, his fingers stretching into his thin hair. He longed for a drink of whiskey…the desire for it grew until it occupied every sensation in his body, every thought in every crevice of his brain.

"Oh, God…help me…"

Then his gaze fell on the small piece of paper that Daisy had thrust into his hand earlier. He picked it up. The title, scrawled in a childish hand, read *Come, My Little Angel*. Beneath the title, she had printed the words:

Mister Taggart,

    This is the song for my drama show. It is about the legend of the littlest angel a little boy who dies and goes to heaven and does not have a gift for the newborn Christ child. Here are the words I wrote so far for my song:

> Come, my littlest angel,
> Is your hallo on strait?
> Boy with a robin's egg
> With a butterfly's wing
> With two shining stones.
> And a hank of puppy hair.

    Well, that's all I have got for now. Maybe you can think of some other words to go with these.

    Your friend,

    Daisy

    P.S. If you think these are queer words for a song, it's because these are the greatest treasures the little angel has. His most-precious-ever possessions. 'Cause he's just a little boy who's come to heaven unexpected like and it's all he has to give the newborned king.

Still supporting his head with one hand, Percival let his opposite hand fall to the piano keys. He brushed them with the pads of his fingers, enjoying the feel of the worn ivories. He played a few chords, mouthing the words to the song. His fingers seemed to move on their own, as if they already knew his heart.

A melody, childlike and sweet, filled his mind. His thoughts calmed as the beauty of the music echoed through the room. He straightened his back and squared his shoulders, frowning in concentration.

He hummed the words, surprised at how beautifully the simple lyrics written by a child fit to the music.

Come, my little angel,
Is your halo on straight?
Boy of one bird egg...
Of a butterfly...
Two shining stones...
Some puppy hair.

Smiling, he added a music-box countermelody to the tune. Words came to him, for the second verse, then a third. He could almost hear the children singing—the angel choir Daisy had dreamed would sing as they performed her play.

He called to mind the legend she spoke of, that of the child who died. And he pictured this child—the same who would become the littlest angel—standing in the center of the stage, clutching his small box of earthly treasures, embarrassed at his humble gift.

"What do I have that's fit for the King?" the child-angel would ask.

Scribbling notes as fast as the images came to him, Percival pictured the small angel's costume, the crooked halo, the torn and tattered robe. This little one would be pushed away by the other angels who were busy with preparations for the Christ child's birth. He would be prone to mischief, always in trouble with the majestic and awesome angels and archangels. This one would long to return to earth because he didn't fit in.

Percival put down his pencil and let his fingers again travel over the keys as his mind flooded with music, heavenly music.

He closed his eyes and sang again. "Come, my little angel..."

"Mister Taggart."

He opened his eyes and turned at the small voice behind him. Somehow he was not at all surprised to see Daisy James.

"Is that my song?" Her face glowed with pleasure. "'Come, my little angel'?" Her words rushed out in an awe-filled whisper. "Is that it? Is it? Oh, please, Mister Taggart, play it again!"

He lifted his hands to the keys, the wonder of the melody still fresh. "Listen—" he said, then halted.

The image of her mother's face shoved the beautiful lyrics and tune from his mind. The promise he had made crushed the wonder.

With a heavy sigh, he turned to the child and frowned as he closed the keyboard cover. "No, it wasn't your song. You heard wrong. I was just fiddling around. That's all. The words you wrote...well, they just don't fit to music."

Daisy's bottom lip trembled. "They don't?"

He stared into her face, the consequence of what he'd just said hitting him full force. He'd raised her hopes by playing her song, then dashed them again within a few beats of her heart. Why hadn't he been more careful?

He placed her scribbled note in her hands.

"Isn't it any good?" she whispered.

He swallowed hard, wishing for courage he did not have. "It is good," he said after a moment. "Very good." It was the best he could do.

She looked up at him, large tears threatening to spill over her bottom eyelids. "Then why...?"

"There's just no music fine enough to go with such wonderful words."

She was not fooled by his attempt to soothe her feelings. "So we can't do my drama show?"

"No." He thought his heart might twist in two at the look on her sweet face. "No, we can't."

"Because you don't want to help us, do you?"

For a moment he did not answer. The only sound was the soft wail of a breeze through the pines outside the music room. "No," he finally said. "I don't."

And with those few words, something inside him died as surely as the hope in Daisy's eyes.

CHAPTER FOUR

WREN AND CADY were sucking on sticks of horehound candy as they waited for Daisy on the wooden porch of the mercantile. It was not a place they were allowed to loiter, and they perked up considerably as she marched across the town square and stood in front of them.

"What happened?" Cady's eyes were wide, though Daisy figured it was more from curiosity than concern. Cady played with the tip of a springy red curl while she waited for Daisy's answer.

"Mister Taggart said he can't help us. I can't help thinking it's about what Ma said to him—" she shrugged—"though I can't figure out what truck she has with it all." Her heart nearly broke. How could her own ma be behind Mister Taggart's change of mind?

Then she told them about the music Mister Taggart had played to the words she wrote. "It was beautiful. Truly like the music the stars sang together when God created the world."

"Sing it for us." Wren pushed up her eyeglasses, looking wise and in charge. She grabbed the hands of the other two girls, and they headed along Main Street to the path through the pines leading to their homes. Daisy hummed the tune she had heard to the best of her memory.

"Come, my little angel," she sang softly, looking up into the pines. "Is your halo on straight?"

Her friends stopped, concentrating so hard their foreheads creased.

"Sing it again," Wren said. And when Daisy did, the other two joined her. The sounds of their sweet, slightly off-key voices made her eyes smart.

Wren stopped singing right in the middle of a word. "We could do it without Mister Taggart."

"We can't."

The corners of Cady's mouth turned downward. "Well, we could. But no one would want to come see us." She shrugged. "They sure wouldn't pay to see us."

Wren was still lost in thought. "Maybe they would if we could get everybody to help us." She brightened. "Think of it. If we could get the whole town to participate—our mas to make our costumes, our pas to set up a big tent and build a stage…"

Daisy bit her lip, but she couldn't stop a big grin from taking over her face. "And put benches in rows. Lots of benches."

Even Cady was smiling now. "How much money would we get for Daisy's church if we charged two bits a person and everybody in town came to see our drama show?"

Both girls looked to Wren to do the ciphering. Everyone knew she was the smartest fifth-level pupil at Red Bud school. "The population of Red Bud is approximately five hundred people, considering even those living in the backwoods."

Daisy's smiled widened. "If everyone came and paid their money, that'd be a *heap*."

Wren seemed unable to resist a look of superiority. "It would indeed."

Daisy let out a whoosh of awe. "Think how much lumber could be cut with more than a hundred dollars!"

They started walking again, hand in hand. "Wait." Wren halted and narrowed her eyes. "We can't build a tent big enough to hold that many people."

"Then we'll put on more than one performance," Daisy said. "I hear tell they do that in the city. Show the same drama show over and over, and folks still come. Sometimes more than once."

"But where?" Wren was frowning again, obviously calculating more than just the money. "If we have it in a tent and the weather's cold—it *will* be near Christmas—then we can't possibly put it on more than a few times…"

"Maybe we can talk our pas into building the biggest tent ever." Daisy nibbled on the tip of her braid, considering the magnitude of the idea. "Something that would hold dozens of people at a time."

"Like a circus tent," Cady added with a giggle. "That would work. I hear tell The Greatest Show on Earth has a tent that'll hold a thousand people!"

Daisy suddenly stopped dead still. "A thousand?" she breathed. "That *would* work. It really would!" Her heart was leaping inside her chest. "A thousand?"

"Maybe we could write to the Ringling Brothers and get them to contribute one." Cady's eyes were bright with the thought of it all.

Wren lifted a brow. "They're called Ringling Brothers, United Monster Shows, Great Double Circus, Royal European Menagerie, Museum, Caravan, and Congress of Trained Animals." When the other two looked doubtful, she went on. "I did a composition paper on it last year. I also happen to know they are located in Baraboo, Wisconsin."

"That's an awful distance…" Daisy's heart suddenly sagged. "Do you think they would send a tent this far?"

"Doesn't hurt to ask," Wren said.

"Surely folks with a name like that could help us." Cady's voice had taken on a reverent tone. "Maybe they'll see we don't want any of the money for ourselves. It's for a good cause."

The three friends changed direction as if with one mind. They followed the winding path back through the grove of pines to the town square, then down the dirt road and past the tavern to the place where they imagined a large circus tent might fit.

Daisy blinked when they reached the vacant spot of land between the tavern and the schoolhouse. It was a beautiful site for the circus tent. And someday, for a church. "Do you think something that big would fit here?" She gazed up at the tall pines that grew all across the slope of the hillside. "We might have to fell some trees."

"A tent that tall would fit right over them," Cady said.

Arms outstretched, Daisy turned in a circle on a carpet of fallen pine needles. She pictured the sweeping canvas, perched on the tops of poles like graceful snow clouds above the sugar pines.

"A circus tent?" She turned again to her friends. "Do you really think the Ringling Brothers might help us?"

Wren nibbled her bottom lip for a moment, a clear sign she was lost in thought. "There are seven Ringling brothers. Alf, Al, Charles, John, Otto, Henry, and Gus. All we need is to convince one, then he can convince his other six brothers."

Cady laughed. "If I tried to convince my brothers of anything, they'd just do the opposite."

"These are grown-ups," Wren said seriously. "They likely respect each other." She scrunched her forehead. "I'm thinking they'd not be inclined to give us a tent. But we could write and ask if they might loan us one. They've got circus trains that travel everywhere. Maybe they could send it up from the valley on the new railroad grade. Maybe in pieces because it would be so big. We could get our fathers and some of the others to put it together."

Daisy kicked a small pinecone. "If it gets here in time for Christmas.

They'd have to send it right away. Then there's convincing our fathers and all the others."

"I have a better idea!" Cady's eyes were wide. "What if we invite the circus to come to Red Bud, animals and all? Then we could use their tent and be part of the circus!"

Wren sniffed. "The Ringling Brothers would likely look down their noses at a drama show put on by children. A show about little angels, when the audience is waiting for tigers and lions and high-wire acts? I don't think so." Cady and Daisy usually rolled their eyes at Wren's look of superiority. Today, they let it go. "Actually, they *couldn't* do that," Wren continued. "They've got eighty-five rail cars and hundreds of animals. Can you imagine an elephant coming up the steep railroad grade in the back of a boxcar?" She took a breath and rushed on. "And even if they did, they'd likely keep all the money for themselves because of the cost of getting here."

"The company brought up all that heavy equipment for the power houses," Daisy said. "I'd reckon an elephant isn't any bigger than a length of pin stock. As for the other, maybe their hearts are bigger than we think."

Wren's tone was gentle. "You always think that other people have bigger hearts than they really do." She reached for Daisy's hand with one of her own. With the opposite hand, she pushed up her eyeglasses. "Like with Mister Taggart."

And my own mother. Daisy swallowed hard and nodded. "It doesn't hurt to try."

Cady's eyes shone with the adventure of it all, apparently unaffected by Wren's words of caution. "I say we write them anyway. Daisy, you have a way with words. Why don't you write a letter tonight, and we'll all look at it tomorrow. I'll ask my pa to post it for us after school."

The girls walked up the hillside to the dirt road leading back to the town square. Daisy glanced toward their school to her left, just beyond a stand of sugar pines, only to see Mister Taggart stepping out and heading toward them. Normally she would have stopped the others and waited, just to see the smile of greeting on their teacher's face. But today she turned without a word and walked with her friends to the square. She heard the crunch of his shoes on the hard earth behind them. It sounded as if he was in a hurry, perhaps wanted to catch up and walk with them.

Unwilling to face him, she nodded toward a shed behind the tavern. "Ever been in there?" She kept her voice nonchalant.

The other two looked at her quizzically.

Wren shrugged. "Why would we want to?"

Cady laughed. "Likely filled with spiders and ground-squirrel nests."

It came to Daisy in a flash. "I was thinking there might be some plywood for our props. Something we might use for clouds. Cut them out and paint them white..."

"Who's it belong to?" Wren was still frowning at the ramshackle edifice.

"What does it matter?" Daisy did not so much as glance over her shoulder at Mister Taggart as she hurried the girls off the road and down the hillside to the rickety shed. "If we find something good, then we'll find out who owns it."

Caught up in the sense of adventure, the others did not seem to notice that Mister Taggart had now overtaken them and strode by on the road just above the shed.

The shed was directly behind the tavern, but slightly off what Daisy figured was the McGowans' property.

One dusty window faced the backside of the tavern, and a single door hung in a lopsided manner from rusty, broken hinges.

Cady wrinkled her nose. "I don't care what's in there. I'm not goin' in."

But even as she spoke she pushed open the door a few more inches and peered inside. She sneezed three times, then backed away, wrinkling her nose. Moving to the window, she stepped onto an old stump so she could see better, and began describing the dusty bottles of liquor she saw.

Then she gasped. "Somebody's been in here. I see footprints in the dust."

"This is where the McGowans keep their whiskey, silly," Wren said with a sniff. "Of course there will be footprints in and out."

"Come see for yourself," Cady insisted. "Come on over here."

Daisy shrugged and started toward the window to join her friend.

Wren was about to follow, then she cocked her head slightly. "Wait!"

At her loud whisper, Daisy paused.

"Over there. I see some branches moving." Wren pointed to a cedar tree.

Daisy followed her friend's gaze upward. Still standing near the window, Cady fell quiet and turned to find out what they were watching. A murmur of voices carried toward them from a tree at the far side of the tavern.

"Somebody's up there," Cady said, taking a single step. "In that tree."

Wren shot out her arm and caught Cady's hand. "Wait." She put her finger to her lips. "Wait."

Daisy cocked her head, listening. One voice sounded like her brother Alfred's, the other like Grover's. Then there was a higher-pitched voice. Toby, the tavern keeper's son. All three voices were coming from the tree.

The others recognized Toby's voice as well and turned to her, giggles threatening to erupt.

"Toby's climbed that tree!" Cady's voice was a loud, snickering whisper. "Think of it! Toby's in that tree!" She plastered her hands over her mouth, looking ready to burst with laughter.

But Daisy wasn't laughing. Something was not right about this. Why would her brothers be talking with Toby? They had never spent more than a few minutes in his presence. And furthermore, why would they climb a tree with him?

Then she remembered the footprints on the dust-covered planks of the liquor shed and shivered. Surely not!

Curiosity got the best of them all. Daisy and her friends crept silently along the carpet of brown pine needles to the corner of the tavern and peered around, looking into the thick, evergreen foliage of the cedar.

The three boys were sitting in the tree all right, about midway up. A jug of whiskey was hanging by its round, crooked handle from a dead limb just below them. Witless grins were plastered on all three of the boys' faces. Toby wobbled precariously from the limb directly over Alfred's head. There was a glow of pleasure on his face, likely from the attention being given him by the older boys. Or on account of the ol' devil liquor—as Daisy's ma called it. At the same moment, it came to her why her brothers were paying attention to the tavernkeeper's son.

Toby likely had a key to the whiskey shed.

Ashamed, she felt her lower lip tremble and looked away.

Then a voice—a loud and angry voice of authority—called up to the boys from a clump of foliage beneath them.

"You there! Come down!" It was Percival Taggart. Daisy would have known the raspy timbre of her music teacher's voice anywhere. "You! Alfred, Grover! Get down. Help Toby. He looks ready to fall."

Alfred had just unhooked the whiskey bottle from the dead limb, and at the sound of Mister Taggart's voice, he started visibly. The brown glass container dropped as if it were made of lead. It hit a small boulder with a shattering crash and landed so close to Mister Taggart that a spray of the liquid covered his shirt and jacket. The pungent odor drifted toward the place where the girls were hiding.

Daisy choked back a cough until her eyes watered. She covered her mouth and bit her lip to keep from making a sound. But Mister Taggart, Alfred, Grover, and Toby were looking anywhere but at her.

Alfred easily slid past the others and landed with a thud on the ground. He wobbled slightly, then leaned almost belligerently against the rough-hewn boards of the tavern. The silly smile still covered his face as he watched Grover grunt and lean out to grab the branch beneath him.

Just as he reached for it, Toby burped, giggled, then wobbled and sang out that he might just let go if someone would catch him. Two things happened in that same instant: Grover slipped from the branch, and Alfred dove to catch him. The older boy succeeded in breaking his brother's fall, but just as he looked up in triumph, Toby sang out again and let go of his branch.

A whoosh, a thud, and a hoot of Toby's triumphant laughter all sounded at once. For a moment, the huddle of three bodies made Daisy think of a litter of puppies—except for the dusty, flesh-colored faces, human limbs and torsos, and torn, soiled clothes, of course.

"Is anybody hurt?" Mister Taggart stood over the group, looking angry and concerned at the same time.

Alfred looked up from the tangle of body parts, seeming too stunned to answer.

Behind him, Toby McGowan sniffled. "My arm. Ow, ow, ow…" He whimpered and rubbed his forearm. "It hurts!"

Mister Taggart knelt quickly beside the sniveling boy. "Can you bend it?"

Toby shook his head, a big tear now making a shiny trail down his dirty cheek. "It hurts." He swiped at the drip with the back of his opposite hand.

"Aw, you're awright, ain't you, Tobes?" Alfred grinned stupidly at the tavernkeeper's son. "Ain't you?" He bent over with a grunt and hoisted himself to standing. He did not so much as glance as his younger brother.

Toby's round face was pale. He swallowed hard and nodded. "Yeah, I guess so." The boy stood shakily and dusted himself off. "I gotta go." He sniffled loudly in unison with Grover and started to limp away.

"Not so fast, young man." Mister Taggart shot out one arm to halt the boy's advance. "You wait here. I have something I want to say to you. To all of you."

Alfred turned with a sneer. "Whasch that, Mister Taggart? Yer too late if you're fixin' to drink with us." He laughed and tried to catch Toby's eye with a knowing look.

Daisy bit her lip, wanting to rush to Mister Taggart's defense. But Wren's hand was on her arm, holding her back as though she understood Daisy's anguish. Cady, who was on her opposite side, let out a small gasp.

"You boys know better than to pull a stunt like this." Mister Taggart's words were solemn and low. His compassionate gaze took in the miserable-looking Toby, the still howling Grover, then came to rest on Alfred. "And you, young man. You're the eldest! You should have set a better example."

Alfred guffawed, then met Mister Taggart's eyes, narrowing his own. "Just as you, sir, have been to the whole community?" Daisy's big brother swung his arm wide, lost his balance, wavered a bit, then caught himself.

"*I* am not on trial here," Mister Taggart said. "But I'm here to tell you drinking behind a shed can start you down a road you want to avoid." His shoulders drooped. "Now," he continued, his voice soft, "it's time to get you boys home. And I daresay you'll be telling your parents exactly what happened." He paused, looking straight at Alfred. "Because if you don't, I will."

Alfred laughed, then muttered, "As if anyone'd b'lieve you."

The stumbling boys marched toward the road, Mister Taggart bringing up the rear like a picture Daisy once saw in a book of an army sergeant. She let out a pent-up breath once they were out of earshot.

"They're gonna get in trouble," Cady whispered. "Bad, bad trouble."

"Serves them right." Wren sniffed, then looked at Daisy, and said, "Sorry."

Daisy shrugged. "They're my brothers but they deserve to be in trouble after what they did." She pictured the boys arriving home and telling all. Her mother's thin, stricken face came into her mind next, followed swiftly by her father's anger. She shuddered. "I better be heading home."

"We'll walk you," Wren said, taking Daisy's left hand.

Cady grabbed the other and gave it a squeeze. She sighed dramatically. "Well, at least your ma may not be so mad at Mister Taggart now."

A few minutes later as Daisy neared her house, it was apparent that Cady's prediction could not have been further from the truth. The yelps from her ma and banshee hollers from her brothers carried through the pines. But the shouts weren't directed toward her brothers as much as they were toward Mister Taggart.

"You go on, now," Daisy said, her voice subdued. Her heart twisted at the sounds of her mother's fury.

She walked up the path to her front door just as Mister Taggart burst through. The smell of whiskey wafted toward her even before she looked up into his face.

Her ma stood in the doorway, calling after him that he was a drunken fool who was leading her sons down a wayward path—the same that he'd been trodding—straight to the gates of hell.

Daisy's beloved teacher brushed past her without saying a word.

"It's true, Ma," she heard Alfred saying from someplace inside the house. "It was him who beckoned us to come to the shed. We would never have done it otherwise. It wasn't my fault. Neither was it Grover's. The blame is on that ol' drunk, Mister Taggart."

CHAPTER FIVE

DAISY PICKED UP Rosemary who was fussing in her high chair. Joggling the baby up and down on her arm, she turned to watch as her mother laid into her brothers. Rosemary sucked on her fist and started to wail.

"I don't care *what* Mister Taggart said or didn't say." Her ma looked madder than Daisy had ever seen her look before. "You both march upstairs to your bedroom and don't you come down until your pa gets home."

Violet and Clover, bent over homework on the kitchen table, snickered, and giggled behind their hands.

Daisy headed to the breadbox, broke a hunk off the day-old loaf, and handed it to Rosemary. The baby gnawed on the hard crust, happily distracted.

"Ma?" Daisy moved Rosemary to her opposite arm and headed to where her mother stood, hands on hips, looking near tears. "Ma?" she said again, softer this time. Her mother turned, the frown disappearing when she saw Daisy and the baby. "It wasn't Mister Taggart. I saw what happened."

"Don't start now. Don't start in about your Mister Taggart."

"I was there, Ma. Honest. I saw what happened."

Ma lowered her voice so the others would not hear. "He smelled like a brewery. I can spot a drinker a mile away. He's one, child. I'm sorry to tell you, but he's just proven what I've known all along. He can't be trusted."

"But I saw with my own eyes—"

"Child, I know you want to believe the best about people, and that's an admirable trait." Her mother's voice grew kinder, and her eyes misted as she touched the top of Daisy's head. "I know you mean well, honey. But you're not doing Mister Taggart any favors by sticking up for him. Too many folks stick up for the likes of him, bringing down others by coverin' up for them."

"But Ma—"

Her mother's voice was harsher now. "I don't want to hear anything more about this from you, child. You hear?"

Daisy let out a deep sigh and felt the tears well. Finally, she nodded. "Yes, ma'am."

Her ma reached for Rosie, and her expression softened as she cuddled the baby. "You go on out and get your ciphering done now, child."

"Yes, ma'am," Daisy said again, turned to join her sisters at the table, then stopped midstep. "Ma?"

Her mother frowned a warning, but Daisy had to ask.

"Ma? What did you say to Mister Taggart earlier today about my drama show?"

"Your drama show?"

Daisy nodded. "Did he tell you?"

Her mother chewed her bottom lip. "Well, no. He didn't say anything."

Because I asked him to keep it a secret. She smiled, then remembered why she asked. "He was going to help me make my story into a drama show for the children to put on. I gave him my song...a song I wrote just especially for it. Later I heard music, like he'd been fiddling around with a melody to my words." Her mother remained quiet, so Daisy went on. "It was beautiful, Ma. Like something angels might sing."

Her ma was playing with Rosie's hair, and still she did not speak.

"But when I asked him about it, asked about my song, he said he couldn't help me now. Couldn't help me now...or ever. That's what he said, all sudden like. I figured your visit must've had something to do with it."

Her ma peered into Daisy's eyes, and Daisy had the oddest feeling...as though her mother were seeing something there she had not seen before. "Go on now, child. Go do your homework." Her voice was softer, and she seemed to be puzzling over something. "Go on. I'll take care of the baby."

Daisy picked up her notepad and a pencil and headed through the back door to the swing hanging from the big oak in the backyard. The sun was slanting from the west, casting long shadows from the pines. Daisy settled onto the wide wooden plank, fluffed her skirts a bit, and sighed. She looked upward into the gnarled limbs, remembering how her pa had looped the rope over the branch when she was just a tyke. She had clapped her hands and danced beneath the canopy of branches as he fastened the wooden seat between the two lengths of rope.

Her pa had instructed her to sit while he measured the distance from the hard soil to the swing. He wanted it to fit just right, he had said. Just high enough to be a challenge to scoot into, but low enough for her feet to press against the ground to provide the *oomph* to sail into the heavens.

Daisy was the only one of his children Pa had measured that day. It made her certain that he had made the swing just for her. No one else.

She twisted the swing, let it spin and then come to a rest while she kicked the soil and thought about her brothers. It frightened her, what Alfred had done. He had broken some unspoken rule that made her heart twist as tight as she had just twisted the swing ropes. She pondered that rule, not knowing how to arrange it in her mind, so alien it was to her thinking.

That he dared to sneak a drink of whiskey was bad enough. But what puzzled and hurt more than anything was how he blamed it on Mister

Taggart. She bit her lip and stared at the ground, watching a fire ant make its way over a dead pine needle. Her disappointment in Alfred weighed like a rock in her stomach, but her sadness about all that had happened to Mister Taggart since morning made her want to cry.

She thought about her teacher sitting alone in the music room, his head down, his fingers nigh onto floating above the piano keys, the music playing by itself without any help from human hands. He had been humming, then singing, the words to her song. And as she thought about it now, the sound was so beautiful it broke her heart.

Looking up into the tree branches, she considered the angels she thought might abide there. Oh, she knew such a thought was fanciful. But she could not help but hope Ma was wrong...that there were such things as real-life beings sent from God above to help His children.

"God, if you are listening, we need to talk." She frowned as she kept her face tilted heavenward. "This church I'm mindful of is for *Your* children—all of us. Alfred and Grover and Toby." She sighed. "And Wren and Cady. Even the little ones: Clover and Violet and Rosemary. And all the rest, big and small, here in Red Bud."

She sighed heavily once more. "And me, God. Maybe most of all. Seein' as how I've bungled it up, could you help me figure out how to do it right? I don't know if I believe in angels anymore." Her shoulders slumped, and she stared at the little red ant making its way across a stone. "I suppose I don't. That's something for children who don't know any better, and maybe I'm not one of them any longer."

When there did not seem to be an answer that came to her, not even a whisper of a breeze that wiggled the branches overhead to make her think of angels, Daisy looked down at the notepad and pencil. After all that had happened, getting a circus tent seemed unimportant. But she had promised

Cady and Wren she would write the letter.

Halfheartedly, she licked the tip of her pencil and started to write:

Mister Otto Ringling of the Ringling Brothers Great Double
Circus and Congress of Trained Animals
Baraboo, Wisconsin
Dear Mister Ringling,

You and you're brothers do not know me, so please allow
me to introduse myself. My name is Daisy James, and I live in
Red Bud. That is in California where we had a gold rush more
than fifty years ago.

My friends Cady and Wren had an idea to write to you,
and seeing as how I am the one who knows how to string words
together the best—or so they tell me! Ha!—I am the one
picked to compose this letter.

Our town Red Bud needs a church. We have a tavern, a
general store, a schoolhouse, and a company where my pa—
actually all our pas—work day and night that will soon make
elect-tricity by bringing water thrugh pipes called pin stocks. I
reckon I don't know how electricity is made from water. I just
know from what my pa has told me that someday it will travel
all the way from here, way high in the mountains, to the big
city of Los Angeles. I always believe my pa.

I have written a drama show called Come, My Little Angel.
(It's about angels in heaven.) Our teacher was going to help us
put it on in our town near Christmas, but now he's changed his
mind. We plan to charge 25 cents for folks to see it.

Wren and Cady and I are going to put on the drama show

anyway. Our town is made up of five hundred people (babies too) and we figure if we get everyone to come see our show, we will have plenty of money to give our pas so they can build our church.

But we do not have a building big enough for all those people to see our drama show. We could do it outside, but seeing as how it will be near Christmas, the snow might keep folks from wanting to come.

And well, a drama show about angels might not go over so well if we wait untill summer. (Ha!)

Besydes, we need our church now. My big brother got in trouble only today. I saw him behind the tavern drinking wiskey with my other brother and another boy named Toby. That was terible, as you can imagine. But worse than that, he lied to Ma about it all. He got my teacher (the same one who said he cannot help us with my drama show anymore) in trouble too.

As you can see, my brother Alfred needs to learn about God before another ocassion comes along to tempt him and he gets in trouble again. He does not believe in angels. Or God either, I expect, though I would never tell anyone else that.

Well, I must go inside now and help Ma with my brothers and sisters. Thank you for reading this, Mister Ringling.

Your friend,

Daisy James

P.S. Ha I almost forgot to ask. Could we borrow your big circus tent for our play? I figure your animals don't need it in the wintertime, though maybe that's where you shelter them when

they are not acting in a show. I have never seen a circus
before, so I don't know anything about that.

Daisy was just starting to read the letter through to check her spelling,
when shouting from inside the house carried through the windows. Alfred
was yelling again, and their ma was telling him sternly to go back to his
room. Clover was teasing Violet, and Baby Rosie was crying.

Grover was puking.

Daisy wished her pa would hurry home to help Ma. She remembered
the narrow, pinched look of her mother's face, and how her eyes seemed
dull and uncaring. She wondered if Pa had noticed, if he knew that their ma
could not take much more of the bad times.

She placed her lined notepad on a smooth stone beside the swing and
headed to the back door. She would finish the letter sometime before the
sun went down.

Abigail stepped outside the back door, leaving the kitchen to Daisy, who
was stirring the batter for drop biscuits and calling out spelling words to
Clover. Baby Rosemary was banging pots and pans on the floor, and
Violet was shelling peas, standing on a stool near Daisy. Clover labored
over forming her words on wide-lined paper, leaning low over the big
kitchen table.

Honestly, she didn't know what she would do without Daisy. The child
seemed to have a magic touch when it came to her brothers and sisters.

Abigail was sorry she needed Daisy so, needed her capable hands to
help out. Too often she saw the longing in her daughter's gaze when friends
came by to invite her to play. Too often Abigail said no, letting Daisy know
her chores came first, that work was more important than play.

She stepped down the concrete stairs and headed to the clothesline. She had just reached up to take down a pair of Orin's work pants when a flutter of paper caught her eye. Clothespin still in her mouth, she headed toward the swing, then stopped with a frown. Surely Daisy knew better than to leave her homework carelessly fluttering in the wind like that!

She bent over to retrieve it, then held it to the waning light. It was a letter. Addressed to Mister Ringling of Ringling Brothers' Circus.

Frowning, she scanned the first page, at first believing it was Daisy's homework assignment. Then the realization dawned. Her eyes filled as she saw into her daughter's heart. Saw what she was up to with her big dreams, the *drama show*, as she called it, the plans to have her father—all the fathers in town—build a church.

Abigail swallowed hard and, almost angrily, put the letter down before reading page three. She brushed the tears from her cheeks. Daisy's heart was too big. She was bound to be hurt. By this Mister Ringling, who would likely read her letter and throw it in the trash. There would be no tent. No show. That would be just the prelude. Even if, by some divine miracle, the drama show about angels was held, next would come the disappointment about too little money, and fathers too tired, too broke, and too busy to care about building a church.

Life was like that. She was sad that Daisy would soon find it out for herself.

Abigail smoothed her apron and started toward the house. Before she reached for the door, a voice called out to her. She turned and peered into the falling dusk.

Her husband's frame was barely visible in the distance. Until he strode close. That was when she saw Orin's face, its thunderous expression. Her heart sank.

"I've just seen Paddy McGowan!" He gritted the words out between clenched teeth. "It seems his Toby fell from a tree and broke his arm. We owe him for the doctor bill and the stolen whiskey."

"We owe him?" Abigail's hand flew to the place over her heart. "Why?" But she already knew.

"It seems our sons led his down a path of ill repute. Caused him to drink whiskey in a tree. He fell and broke his arm in two places. He might even need surgery."

"But we have no money. No extra money." Tears filled her eyes again.

"That's why I've already arranged for Alfred and Grover to start work tomorrow. They'll work until the bills are paid."

"Oh no, Orin. Please, not both of them. The danger. Think of it. They're so young, especially Grover. Oh, please..." She took a shuddering breath, and laid her hand on his forearm. "Besides, I hear it was Percival Taggart who caused all three boys to stray."

Orin's face was still purple with emotion, darkening even as twilight fell. "They should've stood up to him, if that's the case. They need to be kept too busy to get into trouble."

She lifted her chin. "Be that as it may, Percival Taggart should be made to pay the doctor bills."

Her husband met her gaze with a troubled one of his own. "If you're thinking of going after his job, I'm with you this time. But maybe you'd better make sure he has it long enough to pay off Paddy McGowan."

Without waiting for an answer, he took the back stairs three at a time. "Now where're those boys?"

CHAPTER SIX

PERCIVAL TAGGART WATCHED the fall days pass with a growing sadness. It seemed a pall had fallen upon the little town of Red Bud. Even as the golden leaves fell, exposing the gnarled, barren limbs of the oaks that spotted the hillsides, a darkness fell more severe than that caused by mere shortened days.

"Lord," Percival breathed on more than one occasion. "Have you forsaken us? This village? Its children?" He did not add his own name to his complaint, though an awful chill had invaded his soul in recent weeks. He dared not whisper the same question about himself for fear the chill would deepen when no answer was forthcoming.

He found a verse in the book of Isaiah that he clung to, believing, hoping, and counting on it being true: "A bruised reed he shall not break." *Don't break me, Lord,* he pled. But just as the dark silent skies prevailed, so did the silence in his heart.

The week before Thanksgiving a petition began circulating among the citizens of Red Bud, calling for his expulsion from the school and its music department. He knew who was behind the campaign, and it saddened him. Abigail James's fury touched more lives than just his. The rumors flew. Even he heard the whispers drift through the music room windows from the schoolyard.

Each day he watched the light in Daisy's face dim. His heart was heavy with the certainty that once extinguished completely, the child's flame of hope would be hard to rekindle. Hope squashed, an innocence betrayed...and all by the one she loved more than anyone: her mother. A mother who thought she acted out of love and protectiveness.

The child had stayed after music lessons to speak to Percival the morning after he caught her brothers drinking whiskey in the tree. Tears flowing, she confessed she knew the truth about what happened. She wanted him to stand up for that truth, swearing that she, Wren, and Cady would be his witnesses.

Gently, he told her that the people of Red Bud would believe what they wanted, no matter who said what. God knew the truth, and that was all that mattered. He did not assure her that the rumors about his leaving were not true.

He paid Paddy McGowan for the amount Doc Murphy charged to set Toby's arm. Percival had made it clear that it was a gift, given on behalf of the James family. He knew they could ill afford the expense. He also made it clear that it was not due to his guilt in any way. Surprisingly, Paddy McGowan believed him and told the story all over town.

But no one believed the tavern keeper's words, not when they knew Percival had too often whiled away his hours slumped over McGowan's bar.

With three young girls and the barkeeper as his unlikely champions, he kept quiet about his innocence.

"Why don't you stand up for your honor?" Daisy asked him more than once as she put away her fiddle, lingering after the other children had filed from the room. "Let people know how God changed your life?"

He did not answer her the first time she asked, or the second, or even the last—but her words stayed with him through the cold days of autumn, echoing his own conflict. Who he had once been—unredeemed, unloved (or so he thought) and the lowliest of God's creatures—battled with who he was now: a new man with a changed heart.

How could anyone but himself see the change? *Know* the change? Others judged him by the whole of his life.

It was that very judgment that caused his fear.

Who was he, after all, to stand up for honor? He had been the town drunk far too long. Each day he struggled to keep from sliding back into the gutter. Each day might be the last he would spend sober. And, truth be told, his craving for whiskey never diminished. He wondered if it ever would.

Stand up for my honor? He almost laughed.

But all this was impossible to explain to a child, so he kept his silence. Daily he went about his teaching duties, almost mechanically, it seemed. And at night he prayed for a miracle. For himself. For them all.

Daisy headed from the schoolyard one cold evening a few days before Thanksgiving. She had finished writing the final scene for *Come, My Little Angel* two weeks before, and now planned to begin practice. When the news first spread that she had written to Mister Otto Ringling himself, the excitement rose to a feverish pitch. Children wanted to be with her, thinking she had some kind of magical presence because she had dared to write to someone so elevated.

But when the days passed with no answer, they stopped walking with her on the schoolyard. They stopped asking her to share their lunch pails. Worst of all, no one wanted to be in her play. They began laughing at the notion of such a foolish endeavor.

She went to Miss Penney for help, but her beloved teacher said her sister in Sacramento was expecting a baby the week before Christmas. Sorry as she was, she needed to be with her sister the night of the play.

On the night of the first tryouts and rehearsal, Daisy waited with Cady and Wren near the music room until it was clear that no one was coming. Downhearted, Daisy sat alone long after her friends left for home. Then, with a heavy sigh, she walked slowly along the dirt road, heading toward the mercantile in the center of Red Bud square.

She crossed the wooden porch leading into the unpainted store that doubled as just about everything in town: mercantile, barbershop, post office, and socializing place around the potbellied stove for the older folks in tipped-back chairs. The smell of pipe tobacco filled her nostrils as soon as she set foot in the store, mixing with other scents: barrels of pickles, bushels of freshly picked apples, and bolts of newly delivered calico.

After a longing glance at the glass jar filled with sticks of horehound candy, she smiled up at the storekeeper, Mister Ferguson, who looked across the counter at her through wire-rimmed spectacles.

"Good evening, Mister Ferguson. May I have the family mail?"

He smiled, then turned to limp across the rough wooden floor. "You've got quite a boxful today, little lady." He reached for the James family box, but not before she noticed the four small envelopes, one standing taller than the others, tilting kitty-corner inside.

He teetered back to the counter and placed them in her hands.

Afraid to look quite yet, she clutched them close. Then, holding her breath, she peeked at the envelopes, beginning with the smallest.

"Something important, is it?"

She looked down again at the letters, then her eyes widened, and a smile took hold of her face. "Yes, sir!"

In the left-hand corner of the largest piece was a fancy rendering of a circus tent with the words, *Ringling Bros. The Greatest Show on Earth*. Below it was scrawled in ink, *O. Ringling*.

She brought it close to her chest and sighed with delicious anticipation. It was from him. Really from him! Holding it out again, she drank in the signature—*Imagine it! Otto Ringling!*—almost shivering as she imagined the words inside.

Clutching the four letters to her heart, she ran from the mercantile, down the steps and across Red Bud square. Her braids flew out behind as she raced toward the path in the woods that led to her house. The windows glowed in the twilight, beckoning her to hurry home as she rounded the last corner.

But as she opened the picket gate she halted, breathing hard. She looked down at the letter, turning it one way, then the next. What if it was bad news? She would not want the family watching as she read it, feeling sorry for her and tsk-tsking over her squashed dreams.

Everyone would know that her talk of angels, both real and the play-acting kind, and angel choirs and Christmas drama shows would be nothing more than dreams that did not come true.

She frowned at the letter, then walked slowly around the house to the swing that hung from the old oak tree. Lifting the flat stone that was nearby, she placed the letter beneath it and dropped the stone back into place.

Curious as she was to know what Mister Ringling had to say about sending the circus tent, she would wait until daylight. First thing after breakfast, she decided, and no later—no matter what. As soon as the little ones were fed and their homework done, she would race outside and tear open the letter.

Smiling to herself, she headed for the kitchen door.

Abigail woke the following morning feeling something was not quite right. The house was quiet, unusually quiet. In the predawn hours she would normally hear the subdued voices of Orin and their sons wafting from the kitchen as they boiled coffee and made toast before leaving for the ready room near the company commissary.

Then she remembered. This was the day that Orin was taking Alfred to work in the blasting tunnel. That meant they had headed up the mountain on a cable-pulled cart, up the railroad grade paralleling the pin stocks, while it was yet dark. They were needed at the mouth of the tunnel by the time the eight o'clock whistle blew.

As the older of the two, Alfred had been chosen for the better paying job, while Grover had been put to work sweeping the shavings off the floor in the welding shop. Orin had assured Abigail that the blasting tunnels were safer now than ever before. The company had strict guidelines about such things. Such a responsible position, he had argued, would make a man of Alfred and keep him out of trouble.

Abigail swung her legs over the side of the big iron bed and padded down the hall. Opening the door a crack, she peeked into the girls' bedroom. Daisy, Violet, and Clover were still sleeping soundly in their trundle, their sweet faces pink-cheeked, their hair mussed in the predawn light. From the corner, sucking sounds carried from the wooden crib. Baby Rosemary lay topsy-turvily on the thin mattress, eyes closed, fingers in mouth, a tumble of blanket around her.

Abigail crossed the room, unable to resist caressing the baby's soft curls. For a moment she studied each of the faces of her girls. First Violet's, with the three tiny moles on her cheek, one in the shape of a heart. Then

Clover's, with her sprinkle of freckles and small pointed chin.

Finally she studied Daisy, her heart swelling with love and pride. She resisted the urge to move the long plait that Daisy had flung across her forehead sometime in the night. The child sighed in her sleep and turned slightly. The early morning light touched the profile of her cheek, showing its sweet curve and the seashell contour of her ear.

Too quickly she had grown, this precious daughter.

Abigail stood beside the trundle, gazing down at Daisy for another minute. In years past she loved the early mornings best. It was the time she'd spent alone with God, praying for her babies, for their hours in her care, for the days and years ahead when they would no longer be under her wing.

In those long-ago days she sang lullabies, believing every word about God's watchful care and about angels guarding each one of her babes.

But that was long ago. This was now. Lips clamped tight, Abigail grabbed her old chenille robe from the hook behind her door, stepped into her worn scuffs, and headed outside to the privy. She had taken only a few steps from the back porch when loud rumblings carried down the mountain. The ground beneath her trembled, and she reached for the porch rail to steady herself. Her breath caught as she turned toward the sound, one hand rising to her mouth.

The tunnels were eastward, high on a pine-covered bluff. The sun, yet to rise in the cloudless sky, was just behind a dome of granite above the cliff, causing shadows to fall across the unpainted company houses and the gray, hopeless people of the village below.

Abigail shivered and waited to hear the company's three-blast whistle, signaling *Emergency! All available men to the tunnels!* She had heard it before and grieved for the injured, the dead, and their families even before knowing the details.

Now she thought of her boys—Alfred, with his shock of red hair and streak of mischief; Grover, with his luminous, trusting eyes and gentle ways—and she leaned against the porch rail, squeezing her eyelids tight and thinking she surely might die if anything happened to either one.

She waited one minute, two…three, then gulped a breath and held it. The three-blast emergency whistle did not sound. Four, five, six. Her knees finally stopped their quivering. Seven, eight, nine… She breathed again and continued across the dying winter grass, wishing she still believed in a God who listened to prayers.

Daisy woke just as the sun rose above the granite dome, its winter-sparkling light clear and grand as it streamed through her bedroom window. She stretched and yawned, and sat up and stretched again.

Then she remembered the letter. Being careful not to wake her sisters, she tumbled from the bed, and still barefoot, ran through the house to the back door. She pushed it open and headed to the big oak and the nearby flat rock. She knelt beside the stone and dug for the letter she had placed beneath it.

With trembling fingers, she tore open the envelope and began to read:

Dear Miss James,

I regret to inform you that the seven Ringling Brothers are in Europe at the present time, touring The Greatest Show on Earth. As the nephew of Otto Ringling, I am authorized to act in their behalf, and much as I would like to help, I must tell you that the cost of moving a circus tent across the country by train to your High Sierra backcountry town of Red Bud prohibits The Ringling Brothers Barnum & Bailey Circus from making such a commitment.

I am truly sorry. We wish you the very best in your endeavor.

Regards,

Orville Ringling

Shivering in the winter-morning chill, Daisy blinked back her tears and held the letter scrunched to her bosom. Maybe her dreams would not die if she clutched this last hope close.

"Child?"

Her mother's soft voice came from behind Daisy, and a warm arm encircled her shoulders. She buried her face in Ma's old chenille robe that smelled faintly of pine smoke from stoking the fireplace, and bacon from months of breakfasts.

"Child, child, what is the matter?" Ma murmured, rocking Daisy gently in her arms, both still kneeling on the damp, cold ground.

Daisy gave her ma the crumpled letter. "My drama show about angels..." She sobbed softly. "It can't happen now. It's all over. And the church, and everything..."

Her mother laid her cheek on the top of Daisy's head, and for a moment did not speak. Finally, she said, "Disappointments happen in life, Daisy. But they can make us stronger. Really, child, they can. You need to learn that you can't count on others for your happiness or to make your dreams come true."

"But I prayed it would happen, Ma. I prayed so hard."

Her mother did not answer, and after a moment, she stood and helped Daisy stand in front of her. "Listen to me, baby."

Daisy nodded.

Ma lifted Daisy's chin gently with the crook of her index finger. "You need to be self-reliant. Fend for yourself, so you don't get hurt. Be strong so's no one can ever make you cry again." She had set her mouth in a tight line, looking angry. Daisy figured it was at what had happened about the Ringling Brothers.

"Most of all," Ma went on, "don't dream about things that can't ever happen. Those kinds of dreams are childish and mostly made up of nonsense." Ma sighed heavily, looking old and tired. "I've come to conclude, child, such dreams are just ways to keep a body from being responsible for how life turns out."

She peered hard into her daughter's face as if it were a lesson she wanted to make sure Daisy learned well. "You understand?"

Above them a morning breeze was lifting the pine boughs, causing the delicate needles to flutter and sparkle in the sunlight. A tree full of angels, Daisy had always imagined. But that was when she was but a little tyke. Now she knew better.

"I understand," she whispered.

And she followed her ma into the house without another glance heavenward.

CHAPTER SEVEN

THAT SAME DAY as the children pulled out their fiddles and horns for music lessons, Daisy announced that tryouts and rehearsals for *Come, My Little Angel* would not be held after all due to lack of caring and a place to perform it. Afterward, she sat down in her folding chair and dared not look at Mister Taggart, who had hugely disappointed her. And especially she did not look at Wren and Cady for fear of their pitying expressions.

Through the rest of the hour, she pressed her lips in a straight line to keep from weeping. And when class was dismissed she scurried from the room without a word to anyone. To Daisy's great relief, she saw Miss Penney standing in front of the schoolhouse doorway across the play yard, holding the handbell and looking as if she would ring it any minute.

Head down, Daisy barreled her way across the winter-brown field. She had not gone far when Brooke Knight-Smyth and her teasing friends blocked her path. An odd light in their eyes told Daisy they were in a mean-spirited frame of mind. She swallowed hard and tried to give the older girls a friendly smile.

Brooke tossed her blond sausage curls over one shoulder and laughed as she planted her dainty, leather-booted feet squarely in front of Daisy. "So, you thought the mighty Ringling Brothers might loan somebody like *you* a circus tent?" She exchanged a knowing glance with Edmonda, Cordelia, and Emma Jane, who stood at her elbows.

The four sixth-level girls lorded it over everyone else in school. Daily they flaunted their pretty dresses that had never known a patched hem or darned elbow. Daily they stuck their noses in the air, bragging about the fact that together, their kin owned most of the Western Sierra Electric Company. Not a week passed that they did not remind everyone their fathers had the power to hire and fire all the other fathers.

Brooke studied Daisy with the same curiosity one might examine a bug. "What made you think the circus masters would loan you a tent?" Her tone was singsong. Daisy tried to brush past Brooke, but the taller girl stepped sideways to block her path again. "I asked you a question, squirt."

"None of your business," Daisy said evenly.

"And all this business about believing in angels..." taunted Cordelia, who rolled her eyes at Edmonda.

By now Cady and Wren had caught up with Daisy and planted themselves, one on either side.

"Oh, now we have three little peas in a pod." Brooke laughed and gave another toss of her golden curls. "Three little babies who believe in angels."

"And circus tents sent from a benefactor a continent away," snorted Emma Jane. "Think of it." She snickered. "A tent full of angels! Now, what a sight that would be! Can you imagine?" She doubled over in gales of laughter. "A high top filled with angels. Now, that would be a three-ring circus no one could forget."

"I suppose you've never stopped to consider—" Wren sounded not the least bit doubtful—"that even a high top couldn't hold a real angel."

The girls stopped their laughter and taunts.

"It's true," Wren continued. "Real angels aren't the little cherubs you see in paintings and drawings. Real angels are some of God's mightiest beings."

Edmonda, Emma Jane, Cordelia, and Brooke stared at Wren. Cordelia was the first to find her tongue. "How do you know that?"

Wren shrugged. "Think about it. Do you think God would've had tiny baby angels guarding the ark of the covenant? Or singing together when He created the world?" She laughed. "Babies can't do much more than coo."

"Really." Brooke sneered, obviously not impressed by Wren's knowledge and description.

Wren raised a brow. "Really. And that's not all. He sent Gabriel to tell Mary that she was going to have a baby. Gabriel was so mighty, so glorious, Mary fell to her knees in awe." She laughed softly. "Now, tell me, do you think Mary would do that if a little chubby cherub with golden curls suddenly appeared to tell her she was pregnant with God's son?"

Pregnant? Daisy's face flushed at the forbidden word, but speaking it did not seem to bother Wren.

"Angels are mighty beings. Mightier than we mortals can imagine. Likely so big and powerful and filled with light that we wouldn't be able to stand looking at them," Wren continued. "They're sent to guard us in our ways, but if we ever saw one, we'd likely fall on our faces the way Mary did."

Emma Jane narrowed her eyes. "How come you know all this?"

Wren gave them a superior look. "I just do."

"Her family reads books—all the time." Cady lifted her chin with pride.

"It's true," Daisy managed. "Every night Wren's family sits around the fireplace after supper reading and talking about books and ideas." She had seen the family do exactly that, each one contributing. No ideas were too ignorant, no questions ridiculed. Wren's ma and pa seemed to have all the time in the world for their family. The place between Daisy's nose and eyes smarted as she pictured a room filled with such warmth and love. She blinked before any tears could escape, especially in front of the big girls.

Miss Penney rang the bell, but no one moved.

"I suppose you think you convinced us of something we didn't already know." Brooke gave a final toss of her curls. She looked at Daisy and frowned. "Believing in angels, indeed. And circus owners you thought would loan you a tent. What a baby you are!" Thus declaring, she marched away with her perfect little nose in the air, her friends trailing along behind.

Daisy eyes smarted, and she bit her lip to keep from bawling. As soon as the children in front of her had filed into the schoolhouse, she stepped closer to Miss Penney and whispered behind her hand, "I must go to the privy. May I please?"

Miss Penney gave her a quizzical look. "You've had your recess time to take care of personal matters."

"I'm sorry."

"All right, then. Hurry back."

"Yes, ma'am."

As soon as Miss Penney closed the schoolhouse door behind her, Daisy bunched her skirts with her fists and raced across the play yard and through the rusty gate.

She did not look back, but continued running down the dirt road as fast as her legs could carry her. If she held her pent-up sadness inside one more minute she might surely burst. She ran straight to the hillside next to the tavern and plopped down on a smooth rock. Sitting in the one-room schoolhouse for the rest of the afternoon was beyond her heart's capability. And the bawling-out she knew would come later mattered not even as much as a flea bite.

The pines above her rustled, and leaning back on stick-straight arms, she looked heavenward. The trees stood tall and strong, like giant sentinels,

---

unwilling to bend in the wind but willing to sing.

Daisy had changed, but they had not.

She tried to ignore their music, but it sailed above her, swirled around her, caressed her, comforted her. Closing her eyes, she tried to shut out the sounds of slender branches as they lifted their needles into the breeze. But try as she might to think otherwise, their soft rustling reminded her of angels' wings, as though the magnificent beings hovered above her, watched over her, delighted in her.

At last she gave in to their song, though as the sentinels' highest branches sang in the wind, the sound was full of sorrow, as if echoing her lost dreams. As if they felt every squeeze and ache in her heart.

She bowed her head and wept.

Daisy did not know how long she sat there, her arms circling her knees and her eyes squeezed shut. But the scrunch of feet on the hard, rocky soil behind a stand of pines interrupted her. She turned to see who had followed, surprised at the figure that loped awkwardly toward her.

"What are you doing here?" She frowned at the boy, truly not wanting to be disturbed until her cry was finished.

Toby McGowan looked sheepish, his shoulders a thin droop, his stumbling feet the size of snowshoes. He reminded Daisy of a praying mantis, all big gray eyes and long legs.

"I–I felt bad about what happened with your, ah, y–your drama show." He sighed heavily and shrugged. "I–I wanted to see if you were all right."

At Toby's stutter, Daisy suddenly felt sorry she had been so curt. "I'm all right," she said, her voice softer. "Truly."

He gave her a quick nod and turned to go.

"You don't need to leave. You'll likely get bawled out if you're going back to the schoolhouse."

❋

"H–home, too." He met her gaze, then laughed. "B–bawled out there worse'n Miss Penney c–can dish out." He grinned and stepped closer, almost losing his balance on some slick pine needles. "If it's all right, I'll stay." He sat on a rock several feet away, as if afraid to get too close. "So you got a letter back from the Ringling Brothers?"

Daisy nodded. "Yesterday. But I don't care." She let her gaze drift over his shoulder.

"You got a real letter from the circus?" His stutter had disappeared, replaced by a tone of awe. "A real live circus."

Daisy had been so concentrating on her disappointment, she had not considered that it was truly a wonder that a Mister Ringling cared enough to write back, even if it was not the right Mister Ringling. She nodded. "I suppose that's true."

"Could I see it?"

She laughed and pulled the wadded-up, wrinkled page from her pocket. She tossed it across the distance between them. Toby missed the throw and turned an embarrassed shade of plum as he reached to retrieve it from the ground.

He read the letter slowly, mouthing the words. "Th–that's pretty great," he finally pronounced. "It's got a picture of a circus train and everything. Can I show it around?"

"Since Mister Ringling said no, it's not good enough to show around," Daisy said with a shrug. "But I suppose you can if you want to."

Toby turned an even darker shade. "I'd be obliged."

They sat in silence for a bit. A blue jay scolded from one of the pines. Three others joined in, hopping from a top branch of the tallest pine to a nearby oak.

"I was a-wonderin' something," Toby said by and by. He poked a leaf–

less stick at a pinecone and looked over her shoulder as if studying something in the distance.

"If it's about being an angel in the drama show," Daisy said, making a joke, "the answer's no."

But Toby did not laugh. "Why don't you put on the show anyways?"

Her laugh came out a snort. "If I can't get folks to help out now—not even to come to tryouts—I sure can't get folks to come see it."

He was looking straight at her now. "It's a good drama show, Daisy. I've been listening every day when you and Wren and Cady talk about it in music class. You made up a good story." He looked away again.

"Thank you." His words touched her, though she could not figure out why.

"I think you ought to go ahead. P-put it on, I-I mean."

Daisy started to laugh, then stopped. "You mean just for fun?"

He nodded. "D-don't worry about who comes or who doesn't. Or even who's in it or who isn't." He leaned forward, his large eyes bright with enthusiasm. "Let folks try out. It wouldn't matter if they aren't perfect for the part." He busied himself examining a hole in the toe of his shoe.

"Like for the littlest angel?"

He nodded, still worrying with his shoe.

"I always had it in mind that one of the youngest children at school might play that part. Maybe even my sister Violet."

"Y-you especially don't want someone too t-tall," Toby said. "Or someone who trips all the t-time." He poked at his shoe with the stick. "Or someone who stutters."

"You still want to be the star angel?" The words fell out of Daisy's mouth before she could retrieve them.

He looked up and nodded vigorously. "I'd be the best angel ever! Honest, I would."

For a minute Daisy just stared at boy across from her. She had pictured a much different angel to star in her play, someone dainty with a bell-like voice; someone who could sing. Why, heaven only knew what Toby's singing voice was like! She let out a deep sigh. For all she knew he might screech like a cricket.

She felt a twitch at the corner of her mouth, the first beginnings of a smile. If Toby was the only one who cared about her drama show, then he should definitely have the starring role.

"You can be the angel," she said at last. "The star angel."

He looked at her, mouth open, eyes wide. "Really?"

"Really. But nobody else will likely be in the play. And worse than that, nobody may even come."

He was standing now, grinning ear to ear and looking more awkward than ever. She thought he might clap his hands and dance a jig, so she was glad when he just let his big gray eyes dance. Likely he would have tripped on his snowshoe feet and tumbled head over heels down the hillside into a thicket of poison oak.

Percival Taggart was packing up his music, placing books and stands in boxes, when a tap sounded at the door. His letter of resignation was written, signed, and tucked in his breast pocket. As soon as he cleared the music room of his things, he planned to head to the home of Lester Knight-Smyth, the director of Red Bud's schoolhouse board. He did not have peace about his decision, but he was too tired to fight any longer. He planned to leave Red Bud as soon as possible and not look back.

The tap sounded again, and Percival rose from the piano bench to answer it. Before he had taken three steps, the door pushed open, slowly.

"Toby?" He was surprised to see the boy.

"I-I have a qu-question, M-mister Taggart."

"Come in, come in." He smiled to put the child at ease and nodded to a folding chair. Toby headed toward it, stumbled a bit, then settled onto the seat with a sigh. The chair tilted precariously then righted itself.

Percival sat opposite the boy. "What can I do for you?"

The boy thrust a wadded-up page toward him, biting his lip nervously as he dropped it onto Percival's palm. "I-I thought maybe you ought to see this." Immediately, Toby looked down at his feet.

Percival smoothed the paper, then held it to the light of the window. He frowned as he read, then looked up to meet the boy's gaze.

"This is what prompted Daisy to cancel her play?"

"Yes, sir. Sh-she had hoped for the Ringling Brothers to help with the tent. Maybe even bring some o' their circus animals to help bring f-folks to her drama show. Everybody at school's been talkin' about it. That's what made the letter so hard. Now folks are teasin' and makin' fun of Daisy."

Percival's heart twisted at the thought of such cruelty heaped on Daisy's shoulders, especially considering the disappointment she had already borne. He handed the letter back to the boy.

Surprisingly, Toby did not take it. "I-I wondered if maybe, well, ju-just maybe you might help us."

Percival shrugged. "Toby, there's not much anyone can do at this point. I'm leaving town at the end of this term. I'm sorry. I won't be here if you're asking me to help with the music, with the play's production."

"You're leavin'?" Toby looked at him squarely in the face. "You mean, for good?"

Percival did not answer.

"Because of the things that Red Bud folks are sayin' about you?"

"For a number of reasons." It was impossible to explain it to a child. How would he explain about his disappointments in himself and others? About the fears that plagued him. About stumbling worse that even Toby could imagine. About falling and never getting up again... "It's just for the best."

Toby's lower lip trembled. He tried twice to speak, then finally sat there in sad silence, biting his lip and looking at the floor. "Okay," he finally said with a sigh. "But we'll miss you, Mister Taggart."

Percival stood to gently dismiss the boy. "I'm sorry, Toby."

Toby looked up at him and nodded. "But who will teach me the tuba now?"

"I'm certain a new music teacher will be found."

The child was making his stumbling way to the door. "But not as good as you. You're the only one who ever taught me anything."

Percival thought of the off-key bleats, the sad lack of rhythm in the boy, and felt his own tears threaten. He would like nothing better than to spend the rest of his days listening to Toby's music. And all the others'.

Toby reached the door and hesitated a moment before stepping through. "Ab-bout what I-I was going to ask you..."

Percival leaned against the doorjamb and looked out across the play yard to the schoolhouse and the pines beyond. He sighed...how much he loved this place and its children! His children.

"I-I was gonna ask..." Toby was still gazing up at Percival.

"Yes?"

"You see, I-I asked my pa if'n he and my ma might donate some money for the Ringling Brothers' tent. They said they had a little bit put away and that they would be happy to help out."

The tavern keeper and his wife? Paying for a tent that would bring in money for building a church? Percival grasped a stronger hold on the doorjamb, thinking he might surely fall to the floor in surprise.

"W-what I was a-wondering was if you might help me write a letter to that ol' Mister Ringling." Toby pointed to the letter still in Percival's hands. "That's why I got it—though it took some finaglin' to get this away from Daisy!"

"You planned this all along?" Percival finally croaked.

"Y-yes, sir. So now we know where to send a letter back with the money." Toby's large eyes held a look of gentle pleading even as his cheeks flushed plum. "Couldn't you help us get that t-tent?"

Something inside made him want to tell the boy that maybe it was not too late after all, that maybe dreams did not have to die as long as someone kept them alive. Dreams such as drama shows and circus tents and angels and God's care for them all…

But before he could get the words out, Toby McGowan turned and walked away, his thin shoulders in a slump, his gait slow and awkward, and his nose pointed to the ground.

Percival did not have the courage to call after him.

Besides, what did it matter? He was leaving town. The children, the drama show…none of those things were any longer his concerns, no matter how much his aching heart wanted them to be.

CHAPTER EIGHT

PERCIVAL WATCHED TOBY slump from the schoolyard and disappear down the dirt road. Turning back to the music room, he pondered all the boy had said. Sadly, Toby's parents stood to lose money if they mailed it to the Ringling Brothers circus. Who knew if the Ringling nephew, Orville, was a reliable sort? Might be a flimflam artist, for all they knew. Granted, there was no time to write for verification and get the tent to Red Bud in time for the Christmas play. But neither was it wise to send off a sum of money in the mail.

Besides, the money the McGowans were contributing, though a large sum in their thinking, likely would not cover the cost of sending a single railroad car one hundred miles. Let alone a half-dozen cars, which was what such a massive tent with all its posts and poles might take.

He sat heavily on the piano bench again and plinked at the keys absent-mindedly. Without realizing what he was doing, his fingers—almost as if unattached to his hand or his heart—began to play "Come, My Little Angel."

As he played and hummed, he remembered the first time the melody had entered his thoughts. It had been the same day that Abigail James first came to visit.

Abigail James. He considered her now. How would she feel to know the tavern keeper's family was trying to make her daughter's dreams come true? A dream based on Daisy's memory of the time her ma sang in church.

He hit a dissonant chord, then threw back his head and laughed out loud.

Was this not the way of the Lord? To use the most unlikely people to see His plan to fruition?

Had God not chosen a young peasant girl to bear his Son? Chosen her to bear and raise the child who was God incarnate, the One who would turn the world upside down?

Had God not used a rough-hewn shed for the place of his Son's birth?

And the shepherds on the hillside! Did only the shepherds deserve such a privilege hear the angels? Or did the angels sing to all people on earth that night?

He pondered the amazing thought. Could others have heard if their hearts had been tender enough? Open enough?

Almost unable to bear the glory of the thoughts that rushed like a wild and gentle river into his heart, Percival stood and walked to a window. In the waning light of day, the glow of lights in Red Bud shone through the windows of the plain unpainted houses perched on the hillside and inside the tavern to the side of the square.

His gaze moved to the small shed behind the tavern, then to the bare land next door where Daisy wanted the church to be built, where she planned to set up the circus tent.

She was a simple child with a heart tender enough to hear the whisperings of angels in the trees, a heart big enough to dream big dreams that only God could bring to reality.

Had Daisy been among the simple shepherds that night nearly two thousand years ago, Percival had no doubt that she would have heard the angels' triumphant shouts of joy, their songs of praise, at the birth of the Savior.

Oh yes! And likely, she would have lifted her voice in song with them!

If God could use these simple folk of long-ago to bring about His eternal plan, surely He could use Daisy, the McGowans, and a broken-down old music teacher to set this rough and tumble town of Red Bud on its ear.

Who was Percival Taggart to try to block God's mysterious ways?

He had made it this far without slipping into the gutter again, had he not? Suddenly he felt like laughing.

Oh yes, my Lord and God! I've been so busy looking down and worrying about falling that I haven't noticed how it was You who kept me upright all along.

Miss Penney made Daisy stay after school one hour for three days in a row and write on the blackboard 150 times each day:

I will never leave school again without permission.

After that, Miss Penney made her scrub the blackboard clean, wash the children's slates, and stack all thirty-seven blue-backed spelling books neatly on the corner shelf. Last thing before leaving every day, she clapped together Miss Penney's erasers outside the front door of the schoolhouse until white dust drifted like smoke into the surrounding pines.

But all along, Daisy's heart was fairly bursting with song. She chattered with Miss Penney, who did not seem to mind as long as Daisy kept working while they talked. And she dreamed of her little drama show coming to life.

By the end of the third day, after so much thinking and singing to herself, it truly did not matter if only a few parents were in the audience, or if only a few children turned up for tryouts and rehearsals. It did not even matter that tall, gangly, stuttering Toby McGowan was the star angel. All that mattered was that her heart was soaring to the heavens once more.

She fairly danced out the door when her detention ended, heading down the road to the hillside where the drama show would be held.

Cady and Wren were waiting, sitting on a big boulder, elbows on knees, chins in their hands.

"You'll never guess what Toby's come up with," Cady said with a grin.

"What?" Daisy settled onto the boulder beside Wren. Nothing Toby came up with would surprise her anymore.

Wren nodded toward the whiskey shed behind the tavern. "He's thinking if we work hard to clean that old place out, we could use it for a stable. That's where Mary and Joseph and the baby Jesus will be in the final scene."

Daisy's heart caught and she frowned. "But it's got whiskey bottles in it. I mean, we're talking about the place Jesus was born. It seems, well, sacra...sacra..."

"—ligious," Wren finished for her. "Jesus was born in a stable with farm animals." She wrinkled her nose. "Think about the stink!" With a small grimace, she went on. "Besides, we can clean out the shed and spread hay around. Make it smell nice. No one will ever remember what it's been used for by the McGowans."

Cady's voice was hushed when she spoke. "There's something about the drama show that seems...well, different than anything else we've ever done." She knitted her brow in thought. "Everything's gone wrong. First your ma getting so upset like and bursting in to bawl out Mister Taggart, then him saying he can't help." She sighed. "Then the final straw was that the Ringling brothers can't lend us a tent." She fell quiet. "But since Toby's started helping, it's like he's a...well..." She looked embarrassed and nibbled her bottom lip. "Well, like he's a real angel. Always hovering about trying to watch out for others. Especially little tykes in the schoolyard."

Wren coughed and choked at the same time. "Toby?" Her voice came out in a squeak. "Toby *McGowan?*"

Cady nodded. "Now that Daisy's made him the star angel, it's like he's trying to act like one for real."

Wren rolled her eyes. "He's got a long ways to go. I can't imagine anyone more unangelic." She leaned forward. "There are the real angels who are majestic and filled with light. And there are the baby cherubs painted on Christmas cards. Neither type resembles Toby."

Daisy pictured the boy, all gangly legs and gray eyes. She held up her hand. "It doesn't matter. He's playing the part. That's all. It means a lot to him."

Wren frowned again. "So far we've got Toby as the star angel and the three of us in the choir. No music or instruments." She glanced across at Daisy and waited.

Daisy tried not to dwell on the fact that nobody seemed to care. She smiled gently at her two friends. "We'll hold tryouts tomorrow after school. Whoever shows up will get a part."

Cady leaned forward, looking worried. "What if they're terrible? What if people laugh at us...especially at Toby?"

"It doesn't matter now." Daisy lifted her chin. "We're putting on the drama show anyway. They can laugh if they want, even Brooke Knight-Smyth and the others."

"And they likely will," Wren said. "Get prepared."

"I just don't want them to hurt Toby's feelings," Cady said. "I feel sorry we laughed at him that first time he said he wanted to be the star angel. It's a mighty fine thing to see someone as excited as he is over a part in a drama show."

Daisy stood and reached her hands out to her two friends. "Now," she sighed, turning with Cady and Wren in a slow circle until they stopped and faced the front of the pretend theater. "If we hold our play here just as we'd planned before, we'll put the stage over there." She nodded toward the whiskey storehouse. "Most of the story takes place in heaven, but we'll need the shed for baby Jesus, the manger, and the animals at the end."

"Animals?" Wren's laugh came out a snort. "The only kind we've got up here are mule deer and grizzlies. That would hardly be fitting for something that happened in the Holy Land."

"They'll go right along with an angel that's no more fitting than the wildlife then." Daisy laughed. "We'll just use some cardboard cutouts of sheep and cattle." She pictured it and smiled, looking up into the tops of the tallest pines. "And we'll pray for an Indian summer so's the paint won't run."

"And the audience won't freeze," Cady added.

Wren scrunched her brow. "If we hold the play in the daytime, it will be warm enough to seat everyone out here in the forest. And it's not so far-fetched to pray for warm weather. Our nor'westers don't usually hit till after Christmas. That's a well-known fact about California." She took a few steps forward. "We'll put the stage right where we'd planned to before. And the rows and rows of chairs."

"And we'll fill them, you'll see." Cady's voice did not sound as confident as her words. "We'll have everyone in the play sell tickets. They'll have to promise."

"Twenty-five cents apiece," Wren said. "I'll be in charge of the money, if you like."

"Maybe that's too much," Daisy said. She thought how much flour and yeast that would buy for her ma's bread. "Since we're not planning to use the money to build a church, maybe we should let people come free."

"You don't want to build the church now?" Wren knitted her eyebrows tight.

"It just wasn't meant to be. You said so yourself. If we can't get anyone to be in the play, how can we get anyone to come watch?"

"Let's leave that to decide until after tryouts." Wren grabbed Daisy's left hand, and Cady grabbed the right.

Hand in hand, the three girls marched up the mountainside toward Red Bud square. "Come, my little angel," they sang in unison, "put your halo on straight...boy of one bird egg, of some puppy hair...Come, my little angel..." Almost as one, they straightened imaginary halos and raced along the dirt road called Main Street.

Percival heard the murmurings around school the next morning about the tryouts long before Daisy stood to announce the event in music class.

"This is your last chance—" she tipped her chin—"today following the spelling test. Right out here in the school yard."

"Who's in it so far?" Brooke Knight-Smyth looked innocent enough as she asked, but Percival knew the meanness that was likely behind the question.

"We've got three in the angel choir so far," Daisy said. "And our star, the littlest angel."

"Who are they?" Brooke's tone was demanding and lofty at the same time.

Daisy lifted her chin higher. "Cady O'Leary, Wren Morgan, and me in the choir."

The music class all chattered and sighed and spoke at once. "Who's the littlest angel?" was finally called out by one of the big girls in back.

"Who is it? Who is it?" someone else yelled.

Percival finally cleared his throat and raised one hand. "Let Daisy finish, class! Please! Let's have it quiet."

Daisy's cheeks flushed, but she kept her head held high. "It's Toby McGowan. He's our star angel."

A moment of stunned silence fell over the room, then Brooke snickered. "C-co-come, m-m-my l-l-lit-tle a-a-ang—"

"That's quite enough!" Percival shouted above the laughter.

Toby's head was down, and he looked ready to cry.

"Class, you are dismissed. Brooke, I want you to stay after. The rest of you may wait in the school yard. You will be needed again shortly."

Subdued, his pupils marched toward the door then exited to the play yard. Except Brooke, who stood by the piano, waiting.

He strode across the worn oak floor and looked down at her. "That was mean and uncalled for."

"What was?" She raised a brow and tossed him a haughty look.

"You know what I'm talking about—making fun of someone else's malady."

The girl gave her curls a toss and narrowed her eyes.

"I expected better from you," he continued, ignoring her look of challenge. "You have two choices."

"My father won't stand for this! Especially coming from you, the town dr—"

"Your *father* will not be happy to hear about your behavior. From me or from Miss Penney."

She stared at him without so much as a single blink. "So what are my choices?" Her tone was insolent, but he let it pass.

"You can help Daisy with her play, or you can write a ten-page composition about the feelings of others when they are humiliated with teasing remarks. And you will read it in front of the class."

She stared at him for a moment, then her shoulders sagged. "I'll help Daisy James…but it's not because I want to." She gave an offended sniff.

"That's not all."

Now she was glaring again. "There's something else?"

"You will apologize to Toby. Right now, in front of the others."

"I have to do *both*? Apologize *and* help with the play?"

"Take it or leave it." When she looked down, he knew he had won. "Let's ask the class to return."

"I suppose you're going to make me do that, too."

He smiled. "That's not a bad idea. Please invite your school chums to come in. And do it nicely," he added when he saw her fresh glare.

She marched to the door and flung it open with a bang. "Mister Taggart requires that you all return at once," she said in a lofty tone. "And no dillydallying."

Percival swallowed another smile. "Thank you, Brooke."

The children filed in and stood before him in small silent clusters, looking uncertain. Toby's eyes were red-rimmed, and he sniffled loudly.

"We have two announcements to make," Percival announced solemnly. "Miss Knight-Smyth will make the first."

Brooke stood without speaking for a full minute, nibbling her bottom lip until it turned white. Finally, she stared at the children, keeping her gaze from Toby. "What I did…" She blinked, looking like she might cry from humiliation. Percival had to wonder if she had ever been made to apologize before. She cleared her throat and began again. "Well, what I said to, ah, Toby McGowan a few minutes ago…well, actually I didn't say it *to* him. I was, ah, what I did, I mean…" Her shoulders sagged again, and even her curls seemed to droop.

Percival did not want to help her out of her stew, but he said, "Go on," keeping his voice somewhere between stern and gentle.

With a long sigh, she finally glanced toward Toby, whose cheeks had turned a few shades beyond their usual shade of plum. He stared at the floor.

"I'm trying to say I'm sorry." Now big tears welled in her eyes, and a few sighs of amazement rose from the children standing in front of her. "Toby, I didn't mean to hurt your feelings." Without waiting for the boy's response, she marched to the door, threw it open with another bang, and ran from the music room.

Utter silence reigned. All the children stared at the open door, then slowly, one by one, turned toward Toby.

But he did not seem to realize he was the center of attention. Mouth gaping, he looked after Brooke, who was howling theatrically on the play yard.

"Well, then." Percival smiled at the children as if Brooke's scene were as ordinary as any other they might witness during their school day. "Let's continue, shall we?" When they seemed too stunned to answer, he added, "Now, where were we?"

Daisy raised her hand.

He nodded. "Daisy?"

"You were about to tell us the second thing."

He chuckled. "Oh yes, that." He waved a hand at the chairs. "Please, sit down. This may take a while." He walked to the piano and picked up some papers, shuffled them a bit, then sat on the piano bench and again faced the children.

Still surprisingly quiet, they watched him, openly curious.

"As you may have heard, Daisy James has written a play titled *Come, My Little Angel.*"

Daisy's eyes grew round, and she exchanged a glance with her friends Cady O'Leary and Wren Morgan.

A few of the children acknowledged that, yes, they'd heard about Daisy's drama show.

He shuffled the papers again, then met Daisy's curious gaze.

"We have only a few weeks until the day of the play."

"We...?" Daisy squeaked. *"We?"*

"I have written out the parts, based on Daisy's story. We have a dozen major roles, all speaking. Some are angels, some shepherds, the wise men, Mary, Joseph..."

"And the Christ child..." Daisy breathed softly. "Don't forget Him."

Percival smiled at her again. "I haven't." He turned to the children. "We have songs to learn, ladies and gentlemen. Beautiful lyrics composed by Daisy James. And music I've composed that I hope will live up to her words. We haven't much time, so you will need to practice hard, starting tonight. Tryouts for the speaking parts will begin tomorrow."

Now the children were whispering behind their hands, gazing at him with huge eyes.

"There's one more thing." He waited until he had their full attention. "You may have heard rumors that I am leaving. That a new music teacher will be taking my place at the end of the term."

Their quick nods and worried expressions confirmed he was right.

He turned on the piano seat and, letting his fingers travel over the keys, he settled into the first few chords of "Come, My Little Angel."

Grinning and still playing, he let his gaze rest on his pupils. "That, my children, is simply not true." Throwing back his head, he laughed. "And it *won't* be true anytime soon." He nodded once, hard. "Now, sing with me please." He nodded again to the beat. "One, two, three... 'Come, my little angel...'"

CHAPTER NINE

THE FOLLOWING MORNING Abigail saw Orin and the boys off to work with a quiet anger that simmered to the point of boiling. They were too young, Alfred and Grover, to be kept laboring from dawn till dark. She wanted them in school, so they could better themselves. That had been her agreement with Orin. Now this. One blunder and their lives were forever changed. How could Alfred better himself with a pick in one hand and a stick of dynamite in the other? And how could Grover do anything with his life if he spent it sweeping filings in the machine shop?

She stood at the picket gate and watched until the three figures faded into the ashen dawn.

The boys were restless, too. Each night it seemed worse. Last night Alfred had little to say, he just sat sullen and silent, staring into the popping fire. He brightened briefly when Grover suggested they play a trick on their foreman and trade places. With Alfred's protective mask, Grover had pointed out, no one would be the wiser. Besides, he could hammer sticks of dynamite into the tunnel as well as the next man.

After Orin lectured the two on the ridiculous nature of the jest, they had again fallen into moody silence. Something needed to be done. And quickly.

Abigail turned from the gate to head into the house. Lately it seemed the burden of caring for her children pressed so heavy on her shoulders she scarce could make it through her days.

Reaching for the worn handle at the back door, she pulled the door open and stepped into the kitchen. Daisy stood at the stove measuring coffee into the top of the blue-speckled pot. She smiled at Abigail, all mussed and rosy with sleep, waiflike in her hand-me-down chenille robe and worn nightgown, with a pair of her father's woolen socks sagging around her ankles.

"Use a scant amount, child," Abigail said, nodding toward the coffee-pot. "The can is getting low."

"I know, Ma." The child stirred in another half tablespoonful as she adjusted the damper on the old stove.

"Your sisters are still asleep?"

Daisy nodded. "Even the baby."

"You're up early, honey," Abigail said. "Not that I'm unhappy to have your company."

Daisy turned from the stove to join her mother at the table. "I need to talk to you about something. It's important." There was an expression akin to fear in the child's face, and it surprised Abigail.

"What is it, child?"

Daisy met her gaze and nibbled on the tip of her braid, as if considering what to say next. The only thing she seemed willing to let out was a long, soft sigh.

Abigail's voice was softer when she spoke again. "What is it you have to tell…or ask?"

"It's about Mister Taggart…"

Abigail held up a hand. "I really don't want to talk about Mister Taggart. He'll be leaving Red Bud soon anyway."

Daisy let the plait fall to one shoulder, but she kept her blue-eyed gaze fixed on Abigail's face. "I need to tell you what's in my heart, Ma." The child's voice was soft, and Abigail could not find it within herself to stop her.

Daisy leaned forward earnestly. "He's helping with my drama show. He's not leaving Red Bud. He told us so."

"He may *think* his job is se—" Her tongue stopped its waggling when she saw her daughter's face fall. There were over a hundred signatures on the petition she had handed over to the school board. Though no one knew it, least of all Mister Taggart, he would be asked to resign his position and leave Red Bud before Christmas.

"Ma, he's agreed to help me with the music and help the others with their parts, picking out who should play what. And he's written some beautiful songs."

Her heart twisted. "About angels, am I right?"

"It's the drama show I wrote. The one about the little angel in Violet and Clover's storybook."

Abigail did not want to be harsh with Daisy, but neither did she want to prolong this folderol about the unseen world. She did not believe in heavenly hosts and guardian angels any more than she believed in fairy tales. Life was hard enough without mixing woolgathering into a child's pliant mind. She should have burned the picture book about angels long ago.

"It's going to be beautiful, Ma." Daisy's eyes brightened. "You should hear the music Mister Taggart wrote to my words."

"Don't get your hopes up, child," Abigail said gently. "I remember how disappointed you were after you heard from the Ringling Brothers. I don't want you to be disappointed again."

"Even if no one comes, I don't care." She tilted her chin a bit stubbornly. "It's enough just to hear people speaking my words and singing my songs."

Abigail reached for her daughter's hand. "But you do care, Daisy. I can see it in your eyes."

Daisy swallowed hard. "The only one I care about coming, really, is you."

Abigail squeezed her daughter's fingers. "Child, you must understand that as much as I want you to follow your heart's desire, I would be remiss if I didn't protect your heart from harm."

"But...but there's no harm in this, Ma." Daisy looked ready to cry. "You're telling me you won't come, aren't you?"

What she had to say was harder than that, but it was for Daisy's own good in the long run. She kept her voice gentle. "I mean that Mister Taggart is going to be asked to resign his post, child. I've already talked to the school board. They have looked long and hard at his past record, and they have concluded that it is best for all the children if he leaves at the end of the term."

Big tears filled Daisy's eyes. "No!" she whispered. "It can't be!"

"I wasn't going to tell you, honey, until it was announced at school. But I think it's wise for you to be prepared."

"But why, Ma? Why?"

"There are many reasons, and someday you'll understand. You'll know I did it for you."

Before Daisy said a word, Violet and Clover padded into the kitchen. Clover was carrying Rosemary, who reached for her mama. With a smile of confidence that she was truly doing the right thing for Daisy, for all the children of Red Bud, Abigail stood and gathered the baby into her arms. Sometimes a mother had to make difficult choices, choices that children would not understand until they were grown. It was painful, true, but it was for the best.

"Whath wrong?" Violet slid onto the chair next to Daisy. She reached for her sister's hand. "Why are you cryin', huh?"

When Daisy did not answer, Clover sat on the other side. "Is it about the drama show? Are you still worried nobody'll come to tryouts today?"

"It's not that," Daisy said, sniffling softly. "Mister Taggart saw to it yesterday that everybody will be there—even the sixth-level girls."

Abigail walked to the stove, bouncing Rosie on one arm, and dampered the fire under the coffeepot. "Enough talk about Mister Taggart. It's time to get ready for school."

"But Daisy'th cryin', Ma." Violet sounded ready to cry herself.

"She *never* cries," Clover added. "Never. But she is now."

With that, Daisy stood and ran from the kitchen. A moment later, the bedroom door closed with a bang.

"Get your clothes on, girls," Abigail said evenly. "Hurry, now, or there won't be time for toast and jam."

She fought to keep from following Daisy. She wanted nothing more than to hold her little girl in her arms and let her dream her dreams. Instead, Abigail turned to the business of spooning oats into a small bowl for the baby.

Percival Taggart stopped by the mercantile to pick up his mail from the post office that afternoon, just before music class. Surprised by a thick, official-looking envelope, he slid his finger beneath the seal and read it as he walked down Main Street toward the schoolhouse.

It was from the chairman of the schoolhouse board, Lester Knight-Smyth. At first he thought it might be a reprimand for the stern discipline Percival had meted out on the man's daughter Brooke the day before.

Then he realized it was more than that. Much more, though he had to wonder if making Brooke apologize to the tavern keeper's son in front of the whole class had been the final straw in Lester Knight-Smyth's thinking. And who knew what Brooke told her father about the incident.

Behind the letter were two lined pages filled with signatures. He scanned them with a sinking heart. Nearly every family who had a child in Red Bud school, including those in his music classes, had signed. There was no doubt that the people of Red Bud wanted him to leave.

Even without the accompanying letter from Knight-Smyth, the signatures were sad proof that his time here was done.

He looked up into the thin wintry sky. *Lord, how could I have been so wrong? I really thought this was where You wanted me. Just yesterday, I thought I had it figured out. I thought I knew where I belonged. Now this?*

It had been one thing to think about staying when pondering his own resignation, but the reality of getting sacked was quite another. He must have been addlebrained to think about staying in Red Bud, no matter the opposition.

He trudged on to the schoolhouse, his step heavy, his spirit close to breaking again. He passed the tavern and glanced over at it, suddenly thirsty. So thirsty he thought he might die if he did not stop for a whiskey.

What would one glass hurt? Perhaps it would buoy his spirits, give him courage to face the children today.

For today of all days would be the hardest to live through with his charges.

He would tell the children that he would be leaving after all. And that would be that. He would pack up his music, the instruments, and the stands, just as he started to do yesterday. Only this time there would be no turning back.

His feet carried him straight to the clapboard shed where the boys had stolen the whiskey bottles a few weeks back. He cleaned a spot on the window with his sleeve and peered in.

There they were, lined up in a neat row. Bottle after beautiful bottle of the wondrous, amber liquid. He could feel its sting on his tongue, its warm glow in his throat. Licking his lips, he stepped to the door.

It was padlocked, of course. But that would be an easy enough fix. He reached for his pocketknife, pulled it out, and lifted a single blade outward. With the padlock in one hand, the knife in the other, he hesitated.

Inside, the dark bottles called him. Then he heard small footsteps behind him, rushing, stumbling along the pine needle–covered path. A child, no doubt.

He bit back his irritation. So strong was his desire, he could already taste the amber liquid. It would not release him. He did not want it to.

"Mister Taggart...?" Even with his back still to the girl, he knew her identity.

Shame flooded over him as he turned slowly. "Daisy."

She gazed at him with innocent eyes. "This is the shed I was telling you about. The one where the wise men and angels will find the Christ child."

"That's not why I came here."

"I know."

His thirst for whiskey was gone now, and he looked at the ground, shaking from the intensity of what he had just been through.

"I was looking for you before and I saw you head this direction." She fell quiet, though looking like there was more she wanted to say.

"We should be getting back to the schoolhouse," he said.

"My ma told me something this morning—about that, more than likely." She fixed her gaze on the unfolded letter still in his left hand. "If that's from the school board."

"It is." He shrugged.

"That's what I wanted to talk to you about."

They had walked back up the path to the road, and now turned left toward the schoolhouse. In the distance, the shouts and laughter of the children carried on the wind.

"I wondered," Daisy said, "if the school board might change their mind about you leaving after everybody sees the play."

"After?" he said gently. "Daisy, they mean for me to go now."

"Ma said after the end of the term."

"The fall term is over when school lets out, just before Christmas."

She smiled at him. "But the new one doesn't start until after the holidays. Promise to leave, then maybe after the drama show, the school board will change its mind."

They reached the rusty gate leading into the school yard, and he pulled it open so she could enter. "I will speak to the school board about your request. That's all I can promise."

Her eyes shone bright. "Until you do, can we go on with our rehearsals?"

He did not want to extinguish the flicker of hope in her eyes. "I suppose it won't hurt."

She clapped her hands together and almost danced a jig, right there in front of the rest of his charges. "Tryouts, everybody," she called to the children waiting by the music room. "Come on, let's go!"

Three days later, Hannah Sweet told Abigail the news as they took down their clothes from lines on either side of the picket fence that separated their yards: The board was allowing Mister Taggart to teach music lessons through the month of December. That meant the children's drama show would still be put on. Not only that, *Come, My Little Angel* was the talk of Red Bud. It seemed the children were already selling tickets to the play, Hannah Sweet said with an arched brow. Two bits apiece. And the proceeds, so they said, were to go for building a church.

Abigail yanked another clothespin off the line. Now she understood Daisy's dancing eyes of late. And she did not like it one bit. The child was openly defying her. All this talk of angels and playacting and selling tickets had to stop right now.

As soon as the last pair of drawers was taken from the clothesline, she woke Rosie from her nap and set out for the schoolhouse.

If the school board could not stand up to the drunkard who was corrupting the children of Red Bud, by jiminy, she would do it single-handed.

She marched up the hillside, Rosemary cooing in her arms. The baby's cheeks were pink from sleep, and she made sweet babbling sounds, squealing and giggling from time to time. The faster Abigail walked, the more the baby laughed, as if her mother's stiff marching were tickling her funny bone.

It was downright impossible to remain mad as a wet cat when a baby cooed and patted your cheeks with dainty wet fingers.

On top of that, the nearer Abigail got to the schoolhouse, the more soothed she was by the music that poured from the little room off to the side of the play yard.

Even Rosie stopped her cooing and cocked her head to listen.

The sound seemed to float on the air, soaring upward and joining the whistling of the wind through the pine boughs.

Rosie clapped her hands and chortled in delight, her gaze fixed on the treetops as though she saw something that Abigail could not see.

And from that plain, unpainted clapboard music room, the voices of children rose, some off-key, some loud, some soft, some filled with warmth and light and laughter. But together, the words poured forth in a choir unlike any she had ever heard.

"Come, my little angel, is your halo on straight...bring your gifts so fair...to the One you love...to the King above, He loves you so... Come, my little angel, put your halo on straight..."

Abigail did not know when the tears began to trickle down her cheeks. Or why they flowed at all. She did not believe in angels, or in the King above.

Still, the music wrapped around her heart like a blanket of glorious light, touching every part of her being.

So she stood, transfixed, on the dirt road called Main Street, listening to the children sing, and wondering about Rosie's fascination with the breeze in the treetops.

CHAPTER TEN

ABIGAIL KEPT THE strange occurrence near the schoolhouse to herself, but she pondered it day and night, filled with wonder each time she remembered the melody the children sang that day.

Albeit begrudgingly, she silently allowed the drama show to proceed. A kind of peace was struck between her and Daisy as the days passed, especially as she helped all three girls learn their lines. This business about angels was daft, that was for certain, but it was good for them to exercise their minds with memory work.

The second week in December, only ten days until the performance, the younger girls, as usual, were helping with supper.

"Ma, will you help make the costumes?" Clover counted eight potatoes and lifted them out of the metal bin.

"We can't afford the materials, child. You know that."

"But we have them already." Clover frowned, concentrating as she cut the dark eyes out of the first potato. "They were donated."

"Donated?" Abigail patted a venison roast with crushed wild bay leaves. The meat was a rare treat, taken from the cold storeroom in the cellar that morning. "Who has that kind of money these days?"

"Thome people in town gave uth them," Violet said from the stool where she stood in front of the sink, scrubbing carrots.

"Not just *some people,* silly," Clover said with a sniff. "It was Brooke Knight-Smyth's father and mother who ordered the material from Mister Ferguson at the mercantile."

"Ma, they're beauty-full," Violet breathed, scrubbing a carrot. "Mithus Knight-Thmyth made one as a thample. White flannel, they are. And cardboard for the wingth." She sighed. "With thilver glitter cloth cut in fringeth. And wire halos." She put down the carrot she had been scrubbing and demonstrated with wet hands over her head.

Abigail wondered why Lester Knight-Smyth had changed his mind about Percival Taggart, then pondered how she could find the time to add another task to her day. "I suppose so," she finally said. "Mark me down for three gowns. One for each of you."

"Yippee!" Violet dropped her carrot again and clapped.

"Thank you, Ma!" Clover squealed and grabbed her mother around the waist, giving her a hug. "Thank you! We'll be the prettiest angels in the choir."

"I with Alfred and Grover could be in our drama thow," Violet said sadly and picked up another small carrot. "We've got boy angelth, you know."

Abigail smiled softly. Orin had been hinting lately that the boys' work at Western Sierra might be coming to a close. A few exchanged looks with the boys made her think that a Christmas surprise might be in store.

The boys had been on their best behavior recently and had even taken to reading in the evenings around the fire and speaking of how they did not hanker to spend the rest of their lives in mindless employment.

With that pronouncement only the night before, Abigail had met Orin's eyes over their book-bowed heads. Orin gave her the secret smile she adored and nodded ever so slightly, and she knew what he had known all along. Their boys had learned a much-needed lesson—one that the same number of weeks in school could never have taught them.

"Likely they'll not be in the drama show," Abigail said with rare pleasure flooding her heart. "But I imagine they'll attend." She looked down at the trusting little face that tilted toward hers. "Neither will want to miss hearing you sing."

"I get to do more than that," Violet said. "I get to announth the littlest angel'th arrival in heaven." Her tongue played with the place on her gum where her tooth was missing.

Abigail's heart caught again, and she tousled Violet's hair. "And your brothers will be there to watch. They wouldn't miss it." How, she wondered, had she had ever thought that she would?

Daisy raced in from the drama practice for the upper-level children, letting the kitchen door close with a bang behind her. She pumped water at the sink and gulped the glassful down in just five swallows.

"Child!" her mother admonished. "Slow down."

"Ma," she managed to say, though still out of breath. "Ma! You'll never guess what!"

Violet, Clover, and Ma turned to stare.

Clover was the first to speak. "Is it something about the drama show?" She looked worried. "Again?"

Holding a carrot in one hand, a scrub brush in the other, Violet watched her with large grave eyes. "I thtill get to thay my part, don't I?"

"It's something else entirely." Daisy paused, nibbling on her bottom lip, then grinned at them all. "We have sold thirty-nine tickets!" She danced in a circle, clapping her hands. "That means all those folks are coming to see the drama show." She grabbed Violet's small wet hands, helped her from the stool, and danced in a circle around the kitchen.

Laughing, Clover joined her sisters in their jig, then Daisy noticed Ma was just standing there by the stove, looking uncomfortable. Daisy halted abruptly. "Join us, Ma? Please?"

Her mother fluttered her hands toward her face. "Well now, I can't dance. You go on. Have your fun." She turned back to crumbling bay leaves on a hunk of venison, but a small smile played at her lips.

"I remember when you used to dance, Ma," Daisy said. "And sing, too. I remember when our house was filled with music. I was just a little tyke, but I remember."

Ma did not look up again, and when she spoke her voice held a sigh and the smile was gone. "That was a long time ago, child. A long time ago. I don't remember how anymore. So don't go asking me again."

Later that evening, Percival sat at the piano working on the finale for *Come, My Little Angel* when the first explosion rumbled down the mountain.

He stood abruptly, looking toward the window that faced Red Bud square and the mountain above. He saw a belch of dark smoke expelled from the tunnel before he heard the second blast. This one was powerful enough to shake the windows and cause the floor to move beneath his feet.

The emergency whistle began its bleat seconds later. Three long draws. Silence. Then three more followed. Again and again, the mournful whistle blew, calling all available men to the hillside to bring out the injured. The dead.

"Oh, God," he breathed as he reached for his coat. "Oh, God! Be with them all!"

He raced to the bottom of the steep rail grade that carried men and equipment up to the tunnel each morning. Only one flatbed car at a time could be pulled by cable, and the first had already started up the mountain, filled with rescue workers and Doc Murphy. The screech of metal wheels against the iron track carried downward with the drifting smoke to where Percival stood watching helplessly with the other men. In the background the company whistle continued its eerie three-beat wail.

Shivering, Percival stuck his hands in his pockets and glanced over at the worker standing next to him. "Anyone know what happened?"

The man looked grim. "All's we know is that it was something powerful. Worse than most." He kept his eyes trained on the cable car that was still creeping up the incline. "My brother's in there today. I won't rest till I know he's safe."

"I'm sorry," Percival said. "I'll be going up with you next load. I'll help with the rescue."

Around him families had gathered in whispering clusters, mostly womenfolk and children. At the edge of the crowd stood Abigail James, a baby in her arms, her three older daughters clinging to one another and staring upward toward the tunnel.

He whispered another prayer for the safety of the men in the tunnel, then walked toward Abigail.

She seemed to sense his presence even as she kept her eyes on the car still creaking slowly to the top of the mountain. "My husband and son are up there," she said. Her daughters looked up at him, their faces white with fear.

"They have my prayers."

She turned toward him, a vexed look on her face, then glanced down at her daughters, apparently reconsidering her response. Her expression softened and fear replaced the vexation. "Thank you."

Another rumble came from someplace deep in the mountain, and he held his breath as a fresh plume of smoke rose above the tunnel.

Beside him, Abigail gasped, and her daughters started to cry. "M-my pa'th in there," Violet said, staring upward. "An' my brother Alfred."

"Ma! Ma!" yelled a voice from somewhere in the crowd behind them. "Ma!"

Percival turned to see Alfred winding his way through the fear-filled clusters of families.

"Ma!" He gathered his mother in his arms, baby and all.

But Abigail James pulled back with a frown. "I thought you were in the tunnel." Her face was a mix of relief and worry.

The boy looked at the ground and for a moment kept silent. "Me and Grover decided to play a trick today."

"What trick, boy?" She grabbed his arm. "You tell me now. *What* trick, Alfred?"

"We traded places. We didn't think it would bring any harm. Honest, we didn't." Tears filled the boy's red-rimmed eyes. "Ma, I'm sorry. I didn't know this would happen. I wish it were me up there in the tunnel. Honest, I do…I do!" He swiped at his wet cheeks with the backs of his fists. He bit his lip as if trying not to cry, but his shoulders trembled as he gave his ma a desperate look.

"It was as much Grover's fault as yours, son. When he gets down here, you'll both answer for your prank."

"I'm going after him. Him and Pa," the boy said, moving his gaze to the mountain.

"You'll do no such thing!" Abigail cast a pleading look toward Percival.

He gave her a slight nod. She did not want to lose her husband and two sons to the tunnel. "You need to stay here," Percival said to Alfred. "Someone needs to be here to comfort and help your mother and sisters."

The boy stared at him as if just noticing who was standing next to his family.

"I'm going up with the next group," Percival said. "I'll look for your kin first." He put his hand on the boy's thin arm. "I promise."

But as the ashen dusk mixed with the smoke still spewing from high above the huddled families, the first rescue car had yet to descend for the second load. Rumors began to fly. Some said the injuries must be too great for Doc Murphy to allow the injured to make the trip down in the flatbed car. Others said that the rescuers could not reach the victims to send any down the mountain to the clinic.

For the first time, Percival considered that the men in the tunnel might be trapped deep inside the earth. At the same instant, Abigail turned to him, meeting his gaze above the baby's downy head. Her eyes filled with ragged fear.

"I don't know how to pray," she whispered. "I forgot how a long time ago." She paused, searching his face. "Please...will you...?"

Percival had never prayed in public. He scarce knew how to pray silently, speaking to God about his own needs, and when appropriate, about those of others. He had been praying silently for the men in the tunnel since the first blast.

But to pray aloud, not with just Abigail James and her children hearing him, but anyone else within earshot turning to listen.

He was the town drunk, the man most folks remembered as too flush-faced and rheumy-eyed from whiskey to carry on a decent conversation about the weather, too inebriated to walk a straight line.

How could he call upon God to save their husbands, fathers, brothers? He swallowed hard, still staring into Abigail's face. How could he do it? Wouldn't he shame his heavenly Father by the mere attempt?

Then he glanced down at Daisy's upturned face. She reached for his hand, placing her small fingers in his palm.

That simple, trusting act brought him up short, making his heart feel as though a giant fist had taken hold of it and squeezed. How could he have forgotten? God used the plainest of folks, the simplest of tender hearts, to see His will done…from the peasant girl who bore His Son, to the shepherds who witnessed all of heaven's glory.

How could he pray? No, more to the point…how could he not?

"Yes," he said to Abigail. "Let's pray." With his left hand he reached for her hand, Daisy still clinging to his right. One by one the James children clasped each other's hands until they formed a perfect circle.

A reverent hush fell over the crowd as other mothers and their children pressed closer, hands clasped, faces silent and tearful. Almost as one, they reached for the hands of those standing nearby, until nearly everyone in the crowd had formed circles of their own.

Percival's heart hammered, but as he began to speak, an unnatural calm settled over him. And suddenly…suddenly it was as if no one else stood beside him except his Lord.

"Heavenly Father, though we feel so alone and our hearts are filled with fear, we know that You are here beside us. You have said You will never leave us, You will never forsake us. That when we walk through the fire, the flames will not scorch us, when we pass through the rivers, they shall not overflow us.

"You haven't said fires won't flame up. You haven't promised floods of sorrow and pain will not threaten to overflow our hearts. But You have said that when we pass through such times You will be with us. You have said that we are precious in Your sight—each of us. From the smallest child standing here before You today to each one who awaits rescue on the mountain above us.

"We are Yours, heavenly Father, even those of us who have a hard time believing we are redeemed and beloved. You are the same today and forever, and we remember Your promises now. 'Fear not,' You have said to us. 'Fear not, for I *am* with you.'

"Unworthy as I am to ask it, I believe Your promises, Father. Unworthy as I am to even breathe such a petition, I ask that You guard and protect those in the tunnel right now. Help the rescuers to find each one…"

Around him, the sounds of soft weeping rose in the night air. Daisy was squeezing his hand so tight it brought a fresh ache behind his eyes. And on his other side, Abigail wept openly, murmuring the names of her husband and son, beseeching God to keep them safe.

Abigail James had remembered how to pray.

When Percival said amen, several others standing nearby echoed the word. Abigail turned to him, met his gaze, and whispered, "Thank you."

Daisy bit her lip, watching the first load of wounded descend the mountain. A round moon had lifted into a navy blue sky, causing the tracks to glint silvery in the moon's glow. The figures inside the car appeared as plain as day. She could see it was loaded to the hilt with men standing at one end and others stretched out flat at the other end. She caught a glimpse of Doc Murphy's white beard and fedora.

Still clinging to Mister Taggart's hand as tight as she could, Daisy was afraid to breathe. She strained to see her pa and Grover on that truck with Doc.

The car came to a trembling halt, everyone surged forward at once, crushing and crowding, to get to the injured men.

"I see Orin!"

Daisy's heart leapt at her mother's cry. Ma was standing as tall as nature would allow, pointing. "I do! He's at one end of the car, next to Doc." She caught her hand to her mouth. "Oh, dear. They're bending over one of those stretched out…"

But Ma did not have a chance to finish. Mister Taggart simply parted the sea of folks around them—it was just like Moses did that time in the Bible storybook Daisy once found hidden away in a cupboard.

Folks stood back, seeming to understand that it was a James boy on that car. Grover James and his pa stood there beside a worried looking Doc Murphy.

Daisy choked back her fear, clinging to the words Mister Taggart had prayed as surely as she hung on to his big, warm hand. *Fear not, for I am with you,* Mister Taggart had said, just like it was God Himself speaking straight to Daisy's heart.

They reached the edge of the crowd and stepped into a clearing nearby, where the car was being unloaded. Some of the men climbed down, limping and covered with soot and ash. Others were moaning like they were badly hurt. Around them was a bustle of activity as more workers gathered to travel back up the incline.

Even so, Daisy could see that someone was laying on the flatbed, still as death.

There was another hush as Pa looked up and met Ma's eyes. Something passed between them that made Daisy's heart stand still.

It was a look of helpless sorrow, like Pa was sorrier than a body could ever be.

With a small cry, Ma handed Rosie to Daisy and ran to the flatbed to kneel beside her son.

CHAPTER ELEVEN

MA MADE ALFRED watch over Daisy and the younger girls that night because she and Pa planned to keep vigil at the company clinic. Friends and neighbors, more than Daisy could imagine, stayed with those who had loved ones injured—Cady's and Wren's families, Mister and Missus Knight-Smyth, and Mister Taggart among them. Reluctantly Daisy trudged from the clinic with Rosie in her arms. Violet rode on Alfred's shoulder, staring fearfully at Grover, who appeared to be in a deep sleep on a contraption called a stretcher. Clover wanted to stay at the clinic too, but Ma and Pa insisted they all go home, have supper, and stay out of the chill air.

Hours after the little ones were in bed, Alfred and Daisy still had no news about Grover. At nine o'clock Alfred insisted that Daisy go to bed, saying he would stay awake and keep a vigil of his own.

Daisy woke with a start as the Liberty clock struck twelve. A soft melody carried from someplace in the distance. Angels! She was sure of it. She sat up with a smile, knowing Grover must surely be fit again. After a few minutes of listening to the singing, she crept down the hall to her brother Alfred's bedroom and knocked just outside his door.

"Alfred, can you hear it?" she whispered into the dark. "Voices, like unto angels."

He turned on a lamp, looking momentarily confused, his eyes still swollen from sleep or his earlier crying spell. "You must be dreaming, Daisy girl," he said, stretching. "I don't hear anything." He studied her face for a minute, then swung out of bed. He still had on his work clothes. Only his face looked washed—Daisy wondered if it was from soap and water or tears.

Alfred would be in a truck of trouble for soiling Ma's hard-scrubbed bedclothes with his overalls. But then again, Ma had other things to vex her right now. She might not notice.

"How about some warm milk?" Alfred seemed to want to make up for his recent grumpy ways. "I don't think Ma will mind, do you? There's still plenty left in the bottle for breakfast."

He led Daisy back down the hallway into the kitchen and fanned the coals in the stove. Daisy settled onto a chair by the table. He unlatched the icebox door and pulled out a bottle of milk, pouring a small amount into a blue-speckled pan.

The music still carried on the night breeze outside the house. "I can hear it again," she whispered. "Can you?"

He slumped into one of the bent wood chairs across from her. "Maybe it's your angels singing, Daisy girl."

She knew he was teasing, but his voice was gentle. She leaned on her elbows, resting her chin in her hands. "I think it's coming from the clinic. I was thinking that maybe we could just slip out of the house. I'd like to see for myself what's making the music."

"We can't leave the younguns, Daisy. You know that. Besides, what happens with Grover happens...whether we're there or not."

"Tonight when Mister Taggart prayed, I prayed too." She lifted her chin. "Grover will get well. I just know he will."

Alfred moved his gaze away from hers, and Daisy thought his eyes looked wet. He shook his head slowly. "You don't need to make up stories about the music, Daisy girl, and all this talk of angels."

He turned back to her. "It's not that I don't want you to go. I just know that Ma and Pa would have my skin for sure if I allowed it." He stood to pour the milk into her cup, then carefully brought it back to the table. "Especially if anything happened to you," he added softly.

Outside the music seemed to grow louder. It was better than Christmas caroling, in Daisy's way of thinking. It was the kind of music that made a body so happy it could not sit still in a bright kitchen with a cup of warm milk, even if it wanted to.

"How about if you stood in the doorway and watched while I go? I would only be a minute out of sight. Surely Ma and Pa wouldn't mind that." She nibbled her bottom lip, waiting to see if he might agree. "It's not that far."

He studied her face, then gave her another smile. "You promise you'll peek in on Grover, then come right back home again? Tell me how he's doing?"

She nodded over the rim of her mug, then took another big gulp. "I promise."

He stood and handed her a flour-sack dish towel. "Wipe your mustache, then you can go."

"You'll stand watch?"

He chuckled. "You worried about bears?"

"Not in December," she said with a giggle, knowing he was teasing. He was the one who taught her that animals hibernated.

Minutes later, bundled warm in her heaviest coat and gloves and Alfred's wool scarf, she raced along the moonlit path. At the top of the small hill in front of the clinic, she looked back to see Alfred standing in the doorway, the glow of the kitchen lamplight behind him. It made her eyes water, seeing him like that. Her big brother was back.

She blew him a kiss, then ran as fast as her legs would carry her toward the clinic. She reached the top of a small hill and stopped dead still.

There must have been a hundred people in the clearing, maybe two. Each one held a candle, making the pine forest bask in its glow. At the front of the clinic stood Mister Taggart. He was waving his arms the way he did during music class, and everyone standing with the candles followed along, singing softly to the rhythm he had set, music that sounded like lullabies and rushing waters mixed together.

His voice rose clearer than all the others, a silvery sound that warmed her from the inside out. The music blended with the night breeze and the murmuring pines. And it seemed to lift as high as the heavens and join the spangle of stars.

Before she could move, the clinic door opened and Doc Murphy clomped outside onto the wooden porch. The music stopped as he raised his hand, then nodded at a few of the folks in the front row.

"Ladies and gentlemen," Doc called out loud enough for Daisy to hear. "I want to thank you all for your prayers tonight. As you know, seventeen men were injured in the explosion, a few seriously, others with mere scrapes and bruises. All are glad to be alive."

"What about the serious cases?" someone in the crowd yelled. "Tell us how they're doing."

"Only one will require special attention. And that will be a funeral, unfortunately."

Daisy's heart caught, and she leaned forward to hear who it was.

"And that's the canary," Doc said with a cough that resembled a laugh. "I'm afraid the little fella didn't make it." There was a spattering of nervous laughter throughout the crowd. Doc waved his hand. "You all can go home now. The excitement's over. And tonight, folks, don't forget to thank the good Lord for watching over your loved ones."

Daisy had long worried about the caged canary her pa said was taken in the tunnel each morning to test the air, and she thought it was no laughing matter that it had died. With a frown, she was just turning to run back home, knowing she had outstayed her promise to Alfred, when three figures stepped through the clinic door. Her Ma and Pa had their arms wrapped around Grover, who was limping and grinning to beat the band.

With a holler of joy, Daisy clapped her hands and barreled toward them. Grover let go of their parents long enough to catch her in his arms.

After that night Daisy thought her joy was surely complete. The very next day after Pa and Grover were saved from the tunnel explosion, her brothers were fired—much to their ma's delight—for the trick they'd played by switching places. They were reenrolled in Red Bud school before they could say Rumpelstiltskin and made to promise within an inch of their lives that they would knuckle down and work hard and never take even a whiff of whiskey again.

Everyone in town was talking about Mister Taggart. Even Daisy's ma said she could not get over the transformation in him. After his prayer for the accident victims and their families, and after he led songs at the candlelight vigil, everyone in Red Bud wanted to come to the drama show.

One week before the "play" was to open, as Mister Taggart called the Christmas Eve performance, Wren, Cady, and Daisy counted the money from the ticket sales. Their mouths dropped open almost in unison. They counted it again. And again. It took Grover's old handwagon to pull all the tins filled with two-bit pieces to the mercantile.

Twenty minutes later, proud as she had ever been before, Daisy stood in front of Mister Ferguson at the section of the mercantile that doubled as the bank. Wren stood on one side, Cady on the other. When each of them set a tin canister on the counter, quarters rattled and jangled. They repeated the action until all ten containers were stacked in front of Mister Ferguson.

All three could not stop smiling.

"We would like to make a deposit," Daisy said, her heart thumping harder than it ever had in her life.

Mister Ferguson had put on his green visor, just as he always did when switching from storekeeper to banker. "All right. And how much money will you be depositing in your account?"

Cady giggled. "Well, sir, we have just a wee bit from our ticket sales."

"And how much would that be?"

"One hundred, twenty-two dollars and fifty cents," Wren said, her eyes dancing.

"Well, now." He swallowed so hard his Adam's apple bobbed.

Daisy was not as prone to giggling as Cady was, but she dared not exchange glances with her friend or she might end up rolling on the floor. She hoped he did not swallow that hard again.

"In these here cans?"

The girls nodded. "I'm sure you'll want to recount it," Wren said, "but I think you'll find that we were quite accurate in our count."

Mister Ferguson filled out the paperwork for their deposit, asking questions as he wrote. "And whose name is this account to be under?"

They had already decided, and Daisy lifted her shoulders with pride. "Make the account to read, Red Bud Church in the Pines."

"Church in the Pines?" He raised a brow and peered at the girls from behind his spectacles. "Do your parents know about this?"

The three friends grinned at each other, and Daisy thought her heart would soar. "Yes, sir, they do," she said. "And our pas said they'll help build it with the lumber this money will buy."

Mister Ferguson's mouth was still hanging open.

"It will have a steeple," Daisy said. "And a little rock-lined garden out front."

"We'll have Sunday school picnics in the summer," Cady added. "And Bible drills."

"And choir practice every Wednesday night," Wren said. "And maybe someday a piano and an organ."

Mister Ferguson was still peering at them through the wire-rimmed spectacles. "Well, now. Wonders never cease," he finally said. He kept shaking his head as he wrote more words and numbers on the paper. When he was finished, he pushed the paper toward them. "You'll need to sign your names where the X is. All three of you. Then underneath that, Miss James, you may write 'Red Bud Church in the Pines.'"

After they handed over the tins, he took off his visor and solemnly shook hands with them. "And ladies, with this big deposit, you're entitled to a candy stick anytime you stop in to visit your money." He laughed again and handed them each a stick of tangy-sweet horehound candy.

They thanked him solemnly as he placed the tins of quarters behind the counter, explaining that they would be safely in the vault within minutes. "One more thing," he said just as they reached the door. "Tell your fathers anytime they need someone to help pound nails on your new church, I'm their man."

As rehearsals continued, each day seemed to contain more wonder than the day before. Daisy could scarce contain her excitement. Her pa and brothers helped build the stage near the clapboard shed by the tavern. It was finished just four days before the play. Behind it, nestled among the pines, were rows and rows of benches, enough for five hundred people, already set in place. The children's fathers had taken turns after work leveling the ground so the benches would sit steady.

And the shed itself had undergone a transformation of its own.

Three days before the play, Toby and his father helped Mister Taggart remove the shelves that had once held the whiskey bottles. Mister Taggart brought a small cradle that he had made in his woodshop at home, and Daisy helped fill it with hay from an old livery near the outskirts of town. The shed looked more like the place Christ was born and held a sweet scent like fresh mown grass. The smell of hay was so pleasant that Cady and Wren had gone back to the livery for more to scatter on the floor.

That same afternoon Mister McGowan and Mister Taggart used crowbars to pull the boards off one side of the shed so the audience could see inside.

Toby stood back to admire the look of it. "You would n-never know it w-was once used for w-whiskey."

"A right fine idea." Mister McGowan grinned proudly as he came back to admire it himself. "Better than what it was used for previous."

"It'll be a fine place for baby Jesus," Daisy said softly. "There's just enough room for Brooke and Grover and the cutout animals." Brooke had insisted on playing Mary, and Grover reluctantly agreed to be Joseph when none of the other boys would take the part because of bossy, stuck-up Brooke Knight-Smyth.

Toby nodded. "The three w-wise men will have to stay outside." He grinned. "W-which they might have had to do anyway, seein' as they were on camels and such." His stutter had almost disappeared during the rehearsals, but Daisy worried that his nervousness during the real performance might make it return.

The children were so used to it now that they didn't pay it much mind any more. But the audience might be a different matter. Daisy bit her lip. What if they laughed at Toby? It would not hurt for him to practice even harder. "Want me to help you rehearse your lines?"

He blushed and nodded.

"You mind if I stay and watch?" Toby's father asked. It would be the first time he had seen his son play the part.

Toby turned plum and looked at his shoes. Daisy sighed. If he was this shy in front of his own father, what would he do in front of the whole town?

"Okay—" Daisy smiled at Toby—"let's start where you first get to heaven." She inclined her head to the newly finished pine stage. "Do you want to be the first to try it out?"

By now Mister Taggart had come out of the shed, where he had been working on placing the manger, and stood beside Daisy, brushing hay dust from his hands. And Cady and Wren had returned with the handwagon filled with two bales of hay.

They halted the wagon near Daisy and plunked down on a hay bale to watch.

"Try it out, Toby," Mister Taggart said. "Let us know how it feels to be on a real stage. Don't forget to speak up. The people in the last row need to hear you loud and clear."

Toby nodded, and carefully holding his arm, which was freshly out of its plaster cast, climbed the stairs with his awkward, skinny-legged tread. He turned a small circle smack-dab in the middle of the stage, then halted to grin proudly at his father, then Mister Taggart, and finally, at Daisy.

Gulping a deep breath, he stared at his shoes for a long time. But when he lifted his face, his gaze was fixed on the benches. His lips moved slowly as if he were counting the benches in his mind.

"F-five h-hunderd p-peop-ple?" he squeaked. "There's more'n f-five hunderd f-folks gonna be h-here?"

"Take a deep breath, Toby," Mister Taggart said calmly. The music teacher took four strides toward the stage. "Remember what I said. Breathe in and count to ten. Think about speaking to a metronome, just like we practiced."

Toby nodded, his bottom lip sticking out as if ready to cry, his gaze fixed on the empty benches. A look of terror glazed his big gray eyes. He took a step backward and tripped over his shoelace.

Cady and Wren looked stricken and glanced at Daisy. She wanted to cry for the boy on the stage. Instead, she closed her eyes and whispered a prayer.

"One, two, one, two," Mister Taggart said in a rhythmic beat. "Breathe and count, Toby. Breathe and count."

Toby ripped his gaze away from the benches and nodded to Mister Taggart. "O-one, t-two, o-one, t-t-two." Tears filled his eyes. "I-I c-can't d-do it, after all." His face crumpled, and he flung himself from the stage and raced up the incline to the road.

At the top, he stopped and yelled back, "B-besides—" he sounded like his heart might break—"b-besides, l-look over y-yonder. There's a nor'wester c-comin'. It's c-comin', and s-soon!"

A storm? It couldn't be!

The bright afternoon sun hung well above the horizon, and shadows fell crisp from the pines. A typical Indian summer day. Just like Daisy and her friends had prayed for.

Shading her eyes, Daisy squinted to the northwest. Truly, a bank of clouds *was* building, and the sky was turning a telltale hazy blue-gray. She turned at Mister Taggart, hoping for reassurance that a storm was not expected.

But Mister Taggart had already taken at least three loping strides up the hillside, joining Mister McGowan in pursuit of the star angel.

CHAPTER TWELVE

THE RAIN BEGAN that night, light sprinkles followed by winds strong enough to bend the oak branches double. Pa said it was going to be a big one, and Daisy's heart froze as solid as the hailstorm he said would surely follow.

By the time the kitchen clock struck eleven o'clock, gusts of wind and hail pelted the window beside her bed. She shivered and turned over, burrowing under her blankets, praying the storm would last only the night. *One day more at the most,* she reminded God before drifting to sleep, *but only if necessary. Please, though, make it stop in time for our drama show.*

But when she padded to the window the following morning, her heart fell as she lifted the calico curtain and peeked through. The snow was as deep as her Pa's ankle and still falling in big lacy flakes.

Her sisters hopped out of bed and raced to stand beside her, cheering at the first snowy day of winter, chattering about the snowfall just in time for Christmas, and speaking of making snow-cream with eggs and sugar and milk and Ma's precious vanilla drops. Until they saw Daisy's face.

Clover clapped her hand over her mouth. "Oh no!" She blinked at the blanket of snow, then turned again to Daisy. "Maybe the sun will come out this afternoon. It doesn't look too deep to melt in a single day." She peered nervously through the window again. "Honest."

Violet put her hand in Daisy's and pressed her nose against the cold glass, making two little spots of fog with her nostrils. "Why can't we have it in the thnow? Everybody could dreth warm. It'll be fun."

Rosie cooed and gurgled from her cradle in the corner, examining her wiggling fingers. Daisy crossed the room and lifted the baby into her arms. She changed Rosie's diaper, and bouncing the chortling baby on her arm, followed Violet and Clover to the kitchen. They were talking about how they could make snow angels during Daisy's drama show if the storm did not die down.

Alfred and Grover were already seated at the big oak table with their pa, and Ma stood at the stove stirring popover batter into tins.

Pa smiled at the three girls as Daisy dropped the baby into the high chair.

"The wortht thing 'bout thnow is goin' to the necessary," Violet announced as she sped through the kitchen. She struggled into her boots, hopping and twisting in her hurry. "I gotta go. Real bad!" She snatched her coat and flung open the door. The chilly air barreled through the kitchen.

"I'm going first!" Clover pulled on her coat and tried to push her sister out of the doorway.

"Girls!" Ma warned, then laughed as the little ones raced outside, squealing and throwing snow on their way to the privy.

Daisy settled into a chair with a heavy sigh. Pa reached for her hand. "It won't last forever, Daisy girl."

"The sun can melt this much in nothing flat." Alfred's tone was gentle, just like the night of the tunnel fire. "You'll see."

"There's only two days left," Daisy said. "That's not enough time for it to melt." And freezing nights always came after a snowstorm. Everyone knew that. After a nor'wester even the fat icicles that hung to the ground stayed frozen for weeks.

She tried to keep her lip from trembling and stared through the window beyond her brothers.

"I say we go look for our Christmas tree today," Grover said, sounding too cheerful. "We'll go on snowshoes."

She shook her head, and when she spoke her voice was small. "Pa's always said not to go in the woods when it's snowin' this hard." She glanced at her pa who confirmed it with a sorry nod.

Her shoulders slumped. Only the sun peeking from behind the clouds, shining down on Red Bud, bright and beautiful, would make her feel better.

It snowed off and on that day and again the following night. The next morning, the day before the drama show, Daisy ran to the window. The sun was just peeking over the horizon, scattering dancing lights on the icicles and across the snow.

The *deep* snow! She could tell by where it came on the pickets. It was as high as Violet's knees. The beautiful new stage and all the benches were likely large lumps of snow by now.

With a heavy sigh, she crawled back in her bed and covered her head with her blankets. She stayed there all morning, telling her Ma she felt too poorly to rise.

Normally, Ma would not allow such behavior, but everyone in the household seemed to know how much her heart hurt and made allowances. Even her ma.

Just past noon Abigail donned her woolen bonnet and worn coat and pulled on an old pair of Orin's scarred and scuffed boots. She made do with the large size by wearing three pairs of thick stockings so her heels would not slip.

She'd figured where she might find Percival Taggart, and sure enough, he was there. She heard the music from his piano long before stepping foot on the stoop of the clapboard music room.

His music made her think back to how things had changed since she first burst into his music class, indignant and angry about what the town drunkard was teaching Daisy about things unseen.

And now she was coming for his help.

She raised her hand and rapped a soft sound that seemed nearly lost in the wrap of thick mitten wool and the quiet of the snow all around her.

The music stopped, followed by the scrape of the piano bench scooting backward. A moment later, Mister Taggart opened the door.

He did not appear surprised to find her on his doorstep. "Come in, come in." He smiled, a look that utterly transformed his haggard face. He seemed at greater peace somehow than she had ever noticed before.

She stepped through the doorway. He helped her from her coat, and, while pulling off her mittens, she slipped into one of the children's chairs.

He sat across from her on the piano bench, leaning his elbows on his knees. "How is Daisy taking this?"

"She's sick at heart. So much so she's taken to bed." She looked at the floor for a moment, sick at heart herself on behalf of the child, then raised her eyes to his again. "I've never seen her like this."

He looked worried as he nodded slowly. "Her hopes and dreams have been high—more than any of the other children's."

She felt ashamed. "It seems the more I tried to douse her dreams, the more determined she was to dream them." Abigail stood and walked to the paned window, cleared the moisture from a section of glass and looked out at the snow sparkling in the sunlight. "Somehow the seeds of hope were planted in her heart long ago. No matter what I did—thinking I was protecting her—still that hope grew." She turned to face him. "Now I would give anything to see it again."

"But you're afraid it's gone now?"

Abigail nodded. "If you could have seen her face this morning. A foot of snow smothered her last hope for tomorrow. It was like something died in her eyes."

"You must tell her the truth," he said.

"What do you mean?"

"She said that the reason she wants the town to build this church is so she'll hear you sing again. She remembers a little church with a steeple from somewhere in her early childhood. She also remembers how you stopped singing and laughing and dancing with her—soon after you lost the baby."

Abigail stared at him without blinking. "That's what started all this?"

"Yes." His voice was gentle, understanding. "You must tell her that the real dream in her heart is still alive. You must tell her the music hasn't died."

"Daisy…?"

Abigail tapped on her daughter's doorjamb. All she could see was a tumbled lump of blankets on the child's bed. "Daisy?" She settled onto the edge of the trundle bed, reached for Daisy's shoulder, and squeezed it. Folding back the tattered edge of the bedding, she peered into her daughter's solemn face.

"I must tell you some things," she said. "I reckon I'd like it if you'd sit up so we can talk."

Daisy sat up and leaned back against her pillow. "But I still feel poorly."

"I understand that. But you must listen to what I say."

Daisy nodded slowly.

"All along I've told you that I wanted to protect your heart. That by not dreaming big dreams you'll somehow not ever get your heart stomped on from disappointment."

Daisy's eyes were sorrowful with understanding. Disappointment had already taken hold.

"But I've come to a new conclusion, child."

The little girl did not so much as ask what it was, and it near on broke Abigail's heart that she did not. She reached for Daisy's little hand, hoping it was not too late. "You see, honey, we must dream our dreams. We must keep trying to make them happen. No matter what, we must. Because even when those dreams don't come true, it's all right."

Daisy frowned, keeping her gaze locked on her mother's face.

Abigail squeezed her fingers, and dropped her voice as she continued. "You must keep on trying." She leaned forward earnestly, wanting Daisy's face to light up again with hope. "You must keep trying, child, because someday those dreams will come true. It may not be when you thought they would—God's timing is like that. Sometimes sorrowful and sad things happen to us.

"But when they do, He'll be with us. Just like Mister Taggart prayed the night of the tunnel fire. And there's something else I found about dreams and hope."

Daisy leaned forward, a spark of interest showing in her eyes.

Abigail smiled. "It's maybe the most important thing of all."

"What is it?" Daisy finally asked.

"When those impossible dreams finally do come true, the hole in your heart carved by sorrow will cause you to fill with more joy than you can imagine."

Daisy tilted her head. "Really?"

"And there's one more thing—something I've always told you was true."

"That I can't lollygag in bed all day?" There was a giggle in her voice.

Abigail laughed softly. "Well now. Besides that." She reached for Daisy's long braid, unraveled the plaits, and finger-combed through the silken strands. "I've always said God helps those who helps themselves."

Daisy let out a giggling sigh and nodded.

"I say, you'd better get up to the place you're planning to put on your drama show and get to work."

Daisy sat up like a shot. "Wha——?"

"The others have gotten a head start. Pa's there with Alfred and Grover, all with their snow shovels. Even Clover and Violet are bundled up and ready to go with you to help."

"They think we can clear the place?"

"Pa and Mister Taggart are trying to rig up some barrels full of heated rocks." She shook her head. "I'm not certain how they can get enough together for five hundred people." She shrugged and laughed again. "But you know menfolk. They seem to like to bring about the impossible."

Her daughter's eyes were so filled with wonder that it near took Abigail's breath away. She brushed a few strands of hair from Daisy's forehead. "And while we're going around, getting ourselves and Rosie bundled, I'd like you to do something for me."

Daisy seemed so joy-filled that no question, no pronouncement, could further surprise her.

"Would you teach me your song? The one you made up for the drama show?" Abigail smiled into her daughter's eyes. "I don't recollect quite how to carry a tune. But I'd like to learn."

"'Come, My Little Angel'?" Daisy breathed, looking now as if her joy was truly complete.

"That's the one, child. That's the one."

Daisy thought her heels surely had sprouted wings as she raced with her Ma and the bundled-up Rosie to the place next to the tavern.

From the road above the gentle slope of the hillside, they stopped in astonishment. There must have been fifty people working shovels and brooms. It seemed to Daisy that everyone in the drama show was clearing snow, most with their mas and pas and brothers and sisters. Even Mister Ferguson from the mercantile was busy shoveling a path to the stage. And white-bearded Doc Murphy, his fedora tilted in place, was sweeping snow from benches. The area already was half-cleared.

Nearly unable to stop smiling, Daisy found a shovel and started working next to Cady and Wren, so bundled in their snow clothes she scarcely recognized them. They chattered and sang, rehearsing their songs as they worked while small puffs of steam rose from their lips in the cold air.

After a while, she looked up to see Toby McGowan standing off to one side of the stage, leaning on his shovel. The platform had been cleared of snow, and he appeared lost in thought.

Daisy climbed the stairs to where he stood. "Have you been practicing?"

He let out a troubled sigh. "W-with all these folks doing t-this for us, it makes it harder. L-like they'll be expectin' more f-from us, somehow. Now I wish y-you'd picked someone else."

"I don't," Daisy said, meaning it. "You're the right one, Toby. You have been all along."

"B-but I c-can't say my words right."

"The littlest angel was a boy first. Before he became an angel, I mean. In my way of thinking, he should be more like a boy than an angel. Say the words however they come out." She smiled, trying to encourage him. "Be a boy, not an angel."

But Toby looked more scared than ever. "I s–should n–never have asked you," he said. "B–boy or angel, I–I don't think I c–can do it."

The crew worked for two more hours. Daisy was so intent on the progress they had made that only when the company whistle blew at three o'clock did she notice afternoon shadows stretching out long from the pines and a new crop of clouds springing up in the northwest.

Mister Taggart had just brought in a barrel filled with hot stones, and he and her pa were discussing how the same might work to warm the folks at the performance the next day.

Then someone shouted that it looked like snow coming in again. Sighs of disappointment rose in the near-freezing air. People stopped to lean on their shovel handles to stare at the cloud bank, shaking their heads slowly.

With a sigh, Daisy went back to sweeping snow off the remaining few benches, every so often sneaking a look at the darkening skies.

An hour later, the first new flakes began to fall. But Daisy's attention was not on the snow. For at just about the same time, a distant rumble stopped everyone from working.

Murmurs of wonder erupted, and glances were exchanged.

"The tunnels?" someone whispered. "Not again, surely!"

"No, it's coming from a different direction," Mister Taggart said.

"Over there," her pa said. "Over yonder."

"By the railroad grade," Cady breathed, small puffs of steam rising from her lips.

"It *is* coming from the railroad grade," Wren said. "Smack–dab *on* it!" There was a bubble of joy in her tone.

Daisy turned toward the direction they were looking and tilted her head in wonder. She could not make out anything across the cloud-shrouded canyon and through the falling snow. But she knew the sound of a train's clacking pistons and screeching wheels.

This one sounded different than the train that brought pin stock pieces and generators to the company storeyard. And something else mixed with its whistle. A strange wheezing, tuneful, lilting music that made her want to dance and sing.

A calliope.

"Forever more," she whispered more to herself than anyone else. "I do believe it's a circus train!"

Mister Taggart suddenly threw back his head and laughed out loud. "Well, I declare! I *declare!* That's the most wondrous thing I believe I've ever heard!" He laughed again. "Follow me!" he shouted as he raced up the hill-side to the road. "Follow me, everyone!"

Through the snow they trudged, the entire lot of them, following Mister Taggart like he was the Pied Piper. Past Red Bud square and the mercantile they marched, down the pine-covered trail leading to the equipment storage yard and Western Sierra Electric ready room where the railroad tracks ended.

They burst through a stand of pines just as the ten-car circus train slowed at the end of the track and drew to a halt with a screech and blast of steam. Workers in the yard stood gaping.

Daisy thought her knees might give out right there in the snow, so astonished was she. Apparently, she was not alone. Not a word rose from the group around her as they all took in the bright yellow cars with painted scrolls and animals on the sides. Even Mister Taggart, who was still in the lead, remained silent.

Only the calliope wheezed on from somewhere in the back of the train, somewhere behind some bundles of white canvas and stacks of round poles. Scarce before Daisy could take it all in, the door of the fanciest car opened, and a man in a top hat stepped out.

Standing on the platform at the top of the stairs leading from the fancy car, he nodded to the crowd. He seemed not at all bothered by arriving in the little town of silent, gaping folk somewhere in the Sierra high country, smack-dab in the middle of a snowstorm.

The man swept his hat off and bowed to the crowd. "Greetings, one and all!" His bellowing voice sounded just like Daisy had always imagined a ringmaster might sound. "Orville Ringling here, and I am pleased to make your acquaintance."

Laughing, he looked heavenward at the falling snow. For a long moment he seemed lost in thought, and then, casting his gaze across the still-gathering crowd, he grinned. "And it appears we've arrived just in time!"

CHAPTER THIRTEEN

Christmas Eve

PERCIVAL TAGGART LIFTED his baton, and the small orchestra began to play on the downbeat. The scratchy, off-key fiddles and bleating horns filled the big top with music prettier than any he could imagine this side of heaven itself.

The benches were filled—more than five hundred at last count because of the Ringling people who had come along to set up the tent and help in any way they could. They had taken on the children's project after receiving the small sum from Toby and his family, deciding this would be their Christmas gift to the town of Red Bud.

Percival could not know for certain, but he figured the bills he saw Orville Ringling and the others drop in the Church in the Pines contribution box just inside the tent door would help the church fund considerably.

He smiled at the upturned faces before him, watching the children sawing their fiddles and blowing their trumpets. One more surprise lay in store for them all, but it would have to wait till the final scene.

The overture came to a soft close, and Percival nodded to Violet, who stood off to the side of the stage, awaiting her entrance cue.

The child fisted her long angel robe, lifting it to her knees, and climbed onto the high platform. She grinned out at the audience, not a bit scared to see so many faces.

"There ith a new angel in heaven!" Her cardboard wings flapped and her halo bobbed with each word. "A boy freth from earth who lovth puppy dogth and shiny sthones from bubbling brookth." She waggled her finger. "No, he ithn't an ordinary angel. He'th a troublethome boy who will turn heaven upthide down."

Behind her, among a cluster of painted clouds, stood three more heavenly beings, trying their best to look properly angelic: Wren Morgan, Cady O'Reilly, and Daisy James.

Violet turned to the three. "The new angel will arrive juth in time to help the heavenly hoth thing to the newborn King."

With that announcement, Violet bowed to the audience and trotted offstage, her little chin in the air.

The orchestra played another song, and Percival watched as Toby waited for his turn to appear. He whispered a prayer for the child, hoping that his nervousness would disappear. The music dropped, and the boy clambered to the top of the stairs.

He swallowed hard and stared out at the rows of benches. He seemed too stunned to speak.

Percival held his breath.

"I–I have n–no gift for the King," he finally said, his halo trembling with each stuttering word. He closed his eyes, and Percival could almost see the silent counting. "I am still a b–boy," he finally said, "not yet an angel. Why, I–I haven't yet even earned m–my wings."

Skipping to the mark onstage, he stumbled, then righted himself. He sighed and scratched his head. Loping awkwardly to the opposite side of the stage, he tripped over the hem of his robe.

Then...a small smile appeared in the boy's eyes. For the first time, Percival realized Toby was playing his awkwardness to the hilt. He was *using* his tripping, stumbling...perhaps even his stuttering.

It was perfect.

The audience laughed. Toby McGowen had actually become the child too fresh from earth to know perfect angelic behavior, complete with stumbles instead of floating movements and a stutter rather than perfect language. Everyone loved it. And loved Toby.

The boy grinned happily at Percival as he went on. "I have nothing fit for a king. I have only a box of toys I-I brought with me from home." He shook his head sadly. "How c-could such a King be pleased with these plain and simple things?"

He fixed his gaze on the benches filled with people. "It's only got a hank of hair from my favorite ol' dog, some stones from the brook behind my house." He shrugged. "And a butterfly wing. A couple of robin's eggs. That's all. But they're my best treasures in the world."

Every time the boy came onstage, he grew more confident. He said his lines and acted his part with few stumbles and stutters. When they did happen, each gave his angel character a touch that tugged at human hearts.

Percival watched Daisy's play unfold, listened to the audience chuckle and sigh as the angel choir sang and his charges came onstage to recite their parts.

As it came time to prepare for the final act, he signaled the angel choir to move to the side of the stage nearest the shed. Then after a nod to Orville Ringling, the lights dimmed to near darkness.

The children knew the final song by heart, and once Percival had started them singing, they continued on without him while he slipped to the back of the tent and donned his costume.

Come, my little angel,
Is your halo on straight?
Boy of one bird egg, of a butterfly,
Of some puppy hair, some shining stones.
Come, my little angel...

After a moment the lights brightened, just at the time Percival had directed Orville to raise them.

A spotlight was fixed on the shed that once had housed the whiskey. Inside, Joseph, played by Grover James, knelt beside the manger filled with hay. Because his baby sister Rosemary played the role of the Christ child, he played with the little one's hands as she cooed and chortled. Brooke Knight-Smyth, as Mary, was kneeling on the other side of the manger-cradle, gazing at the baby with a look of wonder.

Orville directed his workers to lift the flaps on the back of the tent, and as the choir sang on, the shepherds trailed in and made their way down the middle aisle toward the holy family.

A collective gasp seemed to rise from the audience as the children led in real sheep, brought by Orville Ringling. They bleated and sniffed the hay as they made their way to the front of the big tent.

After recovering their surprise, the angel choir continued singing.

Come, my little angel,
Is your halo on straight?

The shepherds were in place, and it was time for the wise men to make their way forward. A grinning Orville stepped closer and commanded the three camels to kneel.

Taking a deep breath, Percival climbed up the short ladder and took his

place on the tallest beast. Behind him, he heard Orin James and his son
Alfred laughing as they scrambled to the saddles on their own camels.

Percival ducked and swayed as his camel stepped through the tent
opening. Behind him, Orin and James followed slowly.

The audience gasped again, and then a hushed quiet fell over the place.
Only a few children in the choir remembered to sing. Finally, only one little
voice remained. Not surprisingly, it was Violet.

Come, my little angel,
Ith your halo on thraight?

Orville pulled on the reigns, commanding Percival's camel to kneel.
When Percival's feet touched the ground, he slid from the saddle. Facing the
shed where the baby now lay sleeping, and where Mary and Joseph looked
on with adoring faces, Percival knelt to present his gift to the King.

Bring your gifths tho fair,
To the one you love…

Another hush fell over the crowd as Toby came down the aisle alone,
half-running, half-stumbling. He clutched a small box, filled with his earthly
treasures. The boy's face held a look of wonder, and he almost ran to the
manger to drop his gifts before the King.

For a moment he knelt there, his head bowed. Not a whisper rose from
the audience.

Then one by one, the children in the choir began to join their voices
with Violet's.

Come, my little angel,
Is your halo on straight?

Boy of one bird egg, of a butterfly,
Of some puppy hair, some shining stones.
Come, my little angel…

Percival slipped back across the tent to his little orchestra and lifted his baton. Horns blew, fiddles scraped, and drums thumped offbeat. Toby, halo bobbing, ran over to join his classmates, just as Percival had promised he could.

Grinning ear to ear, he picked up his tuba and joined in, offbeat, blaring. Bleating.

Percival met the boy's gaze with a happy nod. Then he turned to the audience and inclined his head slightly…

The best was yet to come.

From the bottom row of the risers where the angel choir sang, Daisy gazed at the old whiskey shed, transformed by the manger scene inside. Baby Rosemary slept in Brooke's arms with Grover looking on. It did not matter that their costumes were made of their pas' old bathrobes, or that Brooke most likely would be sticking her nose in the air tomorrow.

Only the music mattered… Daisy sang softly with the angel choir as the glow of gas lights brightened. She found where her ma and pa were sitting up close to the front of the big tent. Her pa, still in his wise man robe, looked as proud as punch.

But, lo and behold, her ma was standing…looking for all the world as if she was fixing to move toward the aisle. Daisy frowned. Ma must have misunderstood the ending of the play and figured it was time to pick up Rosie from the manger.

Only Ma did not move toward the old shed where Brooke and Grover kept watch over the baby. Instead, she fixed her gaze on Daisy's face and just kept walking toward the stage.

She did not so much as glance at the audience, Mister Taggart, or the angel orchestra as she headed up the steps and moved across the platform. Her eyes were set on Daisy.

The audience seemed to hush even quieter than before. Only the music of the children singing and the orchestra playing filled the big tent. From the corner of her eye, Daisy saw Violet's eyes grow round as saucers and Clover's mouth drop.

Ma stopped smack-dab in front of Daisy, looking at her with so much pride that Daisy thought her heart might burst. Then Ma took her place in the choir between Daisy and Clover. Violet squeezed in, looking up at their mother, her eyes still huge.

Bring your gifts so fair...

Daisy's ma joined the angel choir, lifting her eyes heavenward—and opened her mouth.

To the one you love...

Daisy stood transfixed. Her Ma was singing! And it was a glory! Her voice, clear and true, rang out so beautiful and rich that Daisy thought she might perish from the wonder of it.

Heart full, mouth grinning so wide she could barely form the words of the song, Daisy looked at her ma. She was staring at the tops of the trees that stood beneath the big top. Daisy followed her gaze. The trees seemed to be bending and dancing as if from a gentle breeze—yet it was impossible for the wind to blow in such a place...

Daisy could not be sure, but it seemed the music of the wind and the pines blended with her mother's sweet, pure singing, and with the voices of the angel choir, making even the bleats and bangs of the orchestra a thing of beauty.

The sounds rose, filling the tent with music more beautiful than the rustle of angel wings or a thousand stars singing at Creation.

Ma cast Daisy a soft glance that said she knew. Oh yes, she knew—and believed!

It was the music of God's love. *It was!*

Beloved friend,

The idea for *Come, My Little Angel* was planted in my heart by an event in my childhood: the building of the only church in town by my father, my uncle, and my best friends' fathers. (The cover image is taken from a photograph of the church my father built.) I hasten to add that the characters and events in this story are entirely fictional—except for the miracle of my hometown church's "birth" in the tiny mountain village of Big Creek, in the Sierra Nevada backcountry. And this, dear friend, was the spark that brought this story to life.

I love hearing from my readers. You can write to me at either of the following addresses:

Diane Noble
P.O. Box 3017
Idyllwild, CA 92549
diane@dianenoble.com

Or you can visit my little corner of the Web at www.dianenoble.com. God bless you and keep you always…and may you lift your eyes heavenward each time you hear the rustle of wind in the pines.

Blessings,

Diane Noble

NOVELS BY DIANE NOBLE

Tangled Vines

Distant Bells

The Veil

When the Far Hills Bloom

The Blossom and the Nettle

At Play in the Promised Land

(WRITTEN AS AMANDA MACLEAN)

Westward

Stonehaven

Everlasting

Promise Me the Dawn

Kingdom Come

NOVELLAS

"Birds of a Feather" in *Unlikely Angels*

"Gift of Love" in *A Christmas Joy*

"Legacy of Love" in *A Mother's Love*

NONFICTION FOR WOMEN

Letters from God for Women

It's Time! Explore Your Dreams and Discover Your Gifts

Multnomah Publishers

The publisher and author would love to hear your comments about this book. *Please contact us at:*
www.multnomah.net/mylittleangel